BIRDLIFE

BIRDLIFE

Jim Flegg

Illustrated by Dianne Breeze

PELHAM BOOKS
London

*To the members of the Animal Club at Boughton Monchelsea
School in Kent, in tribute to their enormous enthusiasm and
with thanks for the enjoyment that we share.*

First published in Great Britain by
Pelham Books Ltd
27 Wrights Lane
Kensington
London W8 5TZ
1986

Text © Jim Flegg, 1986
Illustrations © Dianne Breeze, 1986

British Library Cataloguing in Publication Data

Flegg, Jim
 Birdlife
  1. Birds
  I. Title
  598   QL673

ISBN 0 7207 1660 8

Filmset and printed in Great Britain by
BAS Printers Limited, Over Wallop, Hampshire

Contents

	Preface	6
1	Origins	8
2	The Specialities of Birds	20
3	The Framework for Success	46
4	Food and Feeding	74
5	The Breeding Season	114
6	Diversity	150
	Index	156

Preface

Mankind has been interested in and fascinated by birds for several thousand years. The ancient Egyptians revered the Sacred Ibis, and buried it (by the thousand) in mummified form in the graves of their nobility. Long before the Egyptians, primitive men must have relished birds and their eggs as welcome additions to their diet, as indeed we do today. By the time of the early Greek naturalists – like Pliny—and writers – like Aristophanes (who wrote *The Birds*),—some hundreds of years before the birth of Christ, though special powers were still attached to some birds (for example the Little Owl, *Athene*, symbolic of wisdom) some scientific realization of the complexity of birds' lives was becoming apparent among the mystique. Pliny wrote about the spectacle of migration in considerable factual detail, but still persisted in his view that the Kingfisher built a nest of fish bones (which is more or less true) but then launched the nest on the sea to incubate its eggs during a period of calm weather ordained by the Gods, the so-called halcyon days.

We should not scoff at ideas which now seem apparently ridiculous: Gilbert White, the famous natural historian parson of Selbourne in Hampshire, wrote late in the eighteenth century of the possibility of House Martins overwintering buried in the mud at the bottom of village ponds. Inaccurate as this suggestion undoubtedly is, we remain to this day in a great deal of uncertainty as to the exact whereabouts (presumably somewhere in Africa) of House Martins in the winter. The controversy over whether woodpeckers produce their drumming signals vocally, or by hammering on a resonant surface, was only resolved finally (in favour of the mechanical theory) as recently as the 1930s.

Many Victorian and Edwardian naturalists seem to have had both the leisure and the feeling for long hours of intensive observations of the lives of the birds in their area (though of course there were globe-trotting exceptions). To them we still owe a great deal of our detailed basic knowledge of bird biology and ecology.

More recently, the inventions of bird-ringing and of radar have allowed us much greater insight into bird migrations than was previously possible, and have provided much other valuable information (on life spans and causes of mortality for example), but without yet answering that most important of questions: *how* do birds achieve the miraculous accuracy with which their prodigious migratory journeys are accomplished? Hand in hand with recent advances in our knowledge of human physiology, our understanding of the physique of birds has recently improved greatly: yet again we still do not properly understand the workings of birds' air-sac systems, a unique avian feature cardinal to the success of their high-powered lives.

Thus information on how birds live their daily lives, and about the many and various ways that evolution and adaptation have shaped them to so many successes, comes from a multitude of published sources. These are far too numerous to document in detail, but we should record our thanks to ornithologists past and present for the fascinating outcome of their work. Much of what they have discovered is outlined in the pages which follow, presenting a comprehensive picture of the varied private lives of birds. Even more fascinating to the reader will be the realization, as the pages are turned, that despite the long-term popularity of birds and the enthusiasm for their study, much still remains to be discovered. What greater encouragement could there be for us to increase our interest by trying to understand more, to study a little longer, or to look a little more closely at the birds we so much enjoy just watching.

Jim Flegg

1

Origins

Mystery surrounds the origins of birds. Despite the fact that birds must be the best-known of all groups of animals so far as their present-day biology and ecology are concerned, their fossil record is remarkably poor compared with most other backboned animals – the fish, the amphibians, the reptiles and the mammals. Despite our detailed knowledge of the reptiles, particularly leading up to and spanning the 100 million years of the 'age of the dinosaurs' – a period from which any schoolchild can produce a list of a dozen complex scientific names like *Brontosaurus*, *Triceratops* and the fearsome *Tyranosaurus rex*, and link them with their spectacular owners – the first genuine bird, called *Archaeopteryx*, appears in the fossil record with stunning suddenness.

'Archaeopteryx'

To set the scene against which all animal life, not just birds, developed it is necessary to maintain some perspective of passing time. As the period involved spans in excess of 400 million years since the earliest fossil fish, mere mortals with a lifespan of 'three score years and ten' have considerable problems in grasping the detail of the geological time scale, and the associated biological events. The oldest rock formations that we know of have been dated, using radiometric techniques, at about 3000 million years old, and the first fossils (of invertebrate animals, including primitive sea urchins and starfish, for example) appear in rocks laid down about 570 million years ago. Despite the lack of a bony skeleton, the hard shells and carapaces of these early animals often made superb fossils, readily identifiable and in some cases easy to understand anatomically. Plants, of course, came first (all animal life being ultimately dependent on plant life) and for them the fossil record, though scanty in the earliest stages as plants do not fossilize easily, extends back over 1000 million years. It is possible that apparently organized branching networks of silica found in Precambrian rocks in South Africa and North America, dated at over 2000 million years old, are relics of the first plant life forms on earth.

First know your eras

Geological time is divided into eras. Because there is some uncertainty in the dating techniques, expert opinion varies on their precise beginning and ending, but for our purposes the Palaeozoic era spans from about 600 until 225 million years ago; the Mesozoic era from 225 through until 65 million years ago; and the Cenozoic era from 65 million years ago until the present time. Each era is subdivided into periods, and each period further subdivided, either simply into early, middle, and late sections, or into named epochs.

The simplest approach to grasping these technicalities, which are important to our understanding of birds, is the diagrammatic one shown in the table below. This sets out the relevant section of the geological diary and includes in it the events, and the timing of those events, most relevant to the development of birds.

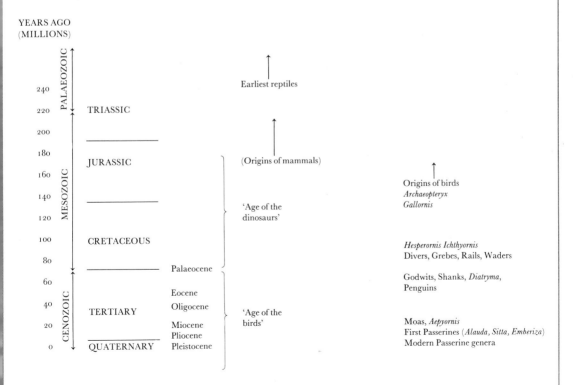

YEARS AGO
(MILLIONS)

240	PALAEOZOIC		Earliest reptiles	
220		TRIASSIC		
200				
180				
160	MESOZOIC	JURASSIC	(Origins of mammals)	Origins of birds
140				*Archaeopteryx*
			'Age of the	*Gallornis*
120			dinosaurs'	
100		CRETACEOUS		*Hesperornis Ichthyornis*
80				Divers, Grebes, Rails, Waders
			Palaeocene	
60				Godwits, Shanks, *Diatryma*,
	CENOZOIC		Eocene	Penguins
40		TERTIARY	Oligocene	'Age of the
20			Miocene	birds'	Moas, *Aepyornis*
			Pliocene	First Passerines (*Alauda, Sitta, Emberiza*)
0		QUATERNARY	Pleistocene	Modern Passerine genera

The earliest bird

The arrival of *Archaeopteryx* in the fossil record is particularly startling because it appears as a more or less normal-looking bird, certainly not as a sort of half-way stage from its reptilian ancestors and not really even all that primitive-looking. *Archaeopteryx* was a true and typical bird anatomically, and externally was clad (like all of today's birds) in a coat of feathers. Even the minute structure of these feathers, formed about 140 million years ago, is closely similar to that of the feathers covering the Starling singing from a twentieth-century television aerial! The only primitive features detectable are the teeth – true teeth, not horny serrations – on the jaws, and the long tail. The tail, unlike the long tails of modern birds, which are purely long feathers, was similar to that of a lizard, fleshy and supported by a long series of vertebrae, but externally covered in feathers, not scales.

Reptile ancestors of the birds

But back to the diary, and the aeons of time prior to *Archaeopteryx* appearing on the scene. The earliest of the reptilian fossils occur in early Triassic times, well over 200 million years ago. Among these reptiles was a group called the *Thecodontia* (known as the 'ruling reptiles' because of their dominance in the ecology of the period) and over the ages it seems most likely that the thecodonts have given rise to the birds. The thecodont skull was really quite bird-like though, as in *Archaeopteryx*, the jaws had conical teeth set in sockets. Many features of the skeleton, too, differ relatively little from those of birds, or at least seem ancestral to them: each vertebra had a concave cup at each end, as in the more primitive birds, and many of the ribs were double-headed, as in birds today. The pectoral girdle – the complex of bones forming the shoulder – was similar to that of birds, especially in possessing a long, slender scapula, or shoulder blade; quite different from the normal stout, broad, triangular bone.

The *Thecodontia* have been divided into four sub-groups, two of which clearly have little to do with the origins of birds. Both of these were heavily armoured (as a protection against predators) and had four legs of equal or roughly equal lengths and short and stout to carry their weight. They obviously walked on all fours. The most primitive sub-group, the *Proterosuchia*, also walked on all fours, but are thought to have given rise to the *Pseudosuchia*, which are of much more interest to students of birds.

A fossil of one of the oldest of the last group comes from the Lower

The wing, however, does show differences from that of a modern bird. The upper arm and forearm in *Archaeopteryx* are in much the same proportion as in humans, and flesh and skin clothed three considerably elongated digits. In modern birds the upper arm is much reduced, while the forearm and metacarpals (the long bones visible in the back of the human hand) are long and carry the flight feathers, the digits themselves being vestigial.

So the skeleton of *Archaeopteryx* shows an intriguing mixture of reptilian and avian characteristics – but any doubts over which group it belongs to must be instantly dispelled by the presence of feathers, which are precisely the same in structure as their counterparts on birds flying today. The strange mixture of characteristics continues into the tail, where typical avian tail feather quills are attached to an equally reptilian tail!

Studies of the fossil skeleton can also give some clues to the bird's way of life. Most strikingly lacking from *Archaeopteryx* are the strong ribs and the powerful, keeled sternum (breastbone) associated with flight. In modern birds, ribs join sternum to backbone to produce a strong box protecting the body organs (see Chapter 3): none such is present in *Archaeopteryx*. Lacking the anchorage necessary for good flight muscles, yet possessing perching feet and well-developed claws on the wings, *Archaeopteryx* probably scrambled about in the vegetation, using its wing claws as does a young Hoatzin in South America today, and flew – in the true sense of beating its wings – rarely, if at all. More likely, it used its wings for gliding from one place to another, much as today's so-called flying lizards and flying squirrels use the skin flaps between their front and back legs. So *Archaeopteryx* may well have looked something like a Hoatzin, or indeed a Touraco.

The evolution of *Gallornis* and *Enaliornis*

The next bird to appear on the fossil time sheet came relatively soon after *Archaeopteryx* – probably only a few million years later. Found near Auxerre in France, it is called *Gallornis*. It resembles more than anything an archaic type of flamingo. It seems unthinkable that in the few million years available the Touraco-like arboreal *Archaeopteryx* could have evolved into a long-legged wading bird like *Gallornis*. The differences between the two are considerable – *Gallornis* also lacked teeth – which implies that as both occurred at the close of the Jurassic/commencement of the Cretaceous period, a common ancestor for them both must be sought a long time back in the Jurassic.

From the fossil record, clearly the Cretaceous was an important period in the evolution of birds. It seems that water birds arose near to the start of the period and expanded considerably during it, becoming more advanced and more diverse as time went on. At this time the global climate was changing, producing new tropical environments in which flowering plants flourished, and it is difficult to imagine that the earliest of land birds were not flying among these flowering and fruiting ferns, herbaceous plants and trees, though sadly as yet we have no fossil evidence of their existence.

Among the earliest of the Cretaceous water birds was *Enaliornis*, found fossilized in the Lower Greensand near Cambridge in 1864 and dated at about 120 million years ago. *Enaliornis*'s skeleton was closely similar to that of living species of our modern diver (or loon) family, of which it was presumably the ancestor.

Diving birds

After a barren period (in terms of discovered fossil remains) of about 20 million years, several new fossil birds appear in the records. Amazingly, eleven species from four different genera have been found in just one locality, in the chalk rocks of Smoky Hill in Kansas, USA. This locality is probably typical of the bed of a sea which at that time extended from the current Gulf of Mexico northwards to the Arctic Circle.

Among these birds were *Baptornis*, which was a flightless diving bird similar in many ways to the grebes of today, one or two species of which have also lost the power of flight in recent times. Another was *Hesperornis*, a diving bird with wings so reduced that it must have been flightless, in some ways resembling *Enaliornis* and modern divers but with sufficient major differences to prove beyond doubt that there was no close relationship. *Hesperornis* had a skull strikingly modified for catching and eating fish: the lower jaws could splay outwards to allow fish of considerable girth to be swallowed with ease, and – most important – at least two of the *Hesperornis* species so far found possessed teeth.

Tantalizingly, among the early fossil birds of which we have any knowledge only *Archaeopteryx* and *Hesperornis* have teeth. In many ways these two birds differ quite strikingly from each other, and from the other birds of the time. It seems likely that teeth were 'on the way out' so far as bird evolution is concerned long before their time, and that

'*Hesperornis*'

Sinbad the Sailor as the Roc that carried off the hero – Arab traders would have been regular visitors to the Madagascan coast. This bird stood some 3m (10ft) tall and, more dramatically, laid eggs which measured about 1m (3ft) round their largest circumference and had a capacity getting on for 10 litres (2¼ gallons). Comparatively speaking, *Aepyornis* has only just become extinct, and its spectacular eggs are still to be found, shallowly buried in recent deposits in Madagascar. It would have been these (Sinbad reputedly took fifty paces to walk round one!) and the huge skeletal remains that impressed the Arabs.

Similarly huge and quite flightless (they had no remnants even of a front limb or wing, nor even a socket on the shoulder for it) were the Moas of New Zealand. These feature prominently in Maori folklore: the largest was *Dinornis maximus*, almost 3m (10ft) high, and they must have represented a valuable food resource to the Maoris. It seems likely it was hunting that eventually drove the Moas into extinction at about the time of the arrival of white men in that part of the Pacific.

The first penguins

The earliest known penguins date from Eocene times. As today, penguins then seemed to be confined almost entirely to the southern hemisphere, and even the oldest fossils discovered show by their skeletal characteristics that they were well-streamlined diving sea birds. The earliest penguins, though, were quite evidently capable of flight, though the wings (like those of the modern northern hemisphere auks) show clear signs of dual use for flying and for underwater propulsion. Only later did the penguins further evolve to become the fully aquatic birds they are today, with the wing adapted as a stiff, powerful, propulsive flipper. The most striking feature of the early penguins was again their size: *Pachydyptes* of the Miocene period was about as tall as modern man and thus about twice the height of the largest living penguin, the Emperor.

Carnivorous birds

Probably the most worrying of these ancient creatures to the time traveller would have been the carnivorous birds. A spectacular example of these is *Diatryma*, whose fossil remains have been found in Eocene deposits in Wyoming, USA. Getting on for ostrich-sized, *Diatryma* was flightless but, like the ostriches, a very fast runner. While most of the ancient giant birds like *Aepyornis* and *Dinornis* had huge legs and feet,

'Diatryma'

bulky bodies but disproportionately small heads, *Diatryma* was equipped with a massive skull and beak, shaped like that of an eagle but perhaps 15–20cm (6–8ins) long and almost as deep! As a predator it must have rivalled most of the carnivorous mammals of the time and filled a role earlier exploited magnificently by some well-known dinosaurs like *Tyranosaurus*, striking fear into all who saw it and capable of running down and killing a wide range of prey.

Adaptive radiation

During the Tertiary period, to judge from fossil remains, there seem to have been two bursts of adaptive radiation, that process whereby the various selective pressures of evolution gradually re-shape the original structure or anatomy of the creature (or just parts of it, like the feet or beak) to fit its new life-style all the better. The earliest, largely in Eocene times (around 50 million years ago), saw the development of the range of water- and shore-bird families familiar to us today (the godwits and the Redshank and its relatives date from this time), and the non-passerine avifaunas of forest, scrub and plains also came into being. The second period of radiation into new habitats or new niches within those habitats occurred during the Miocene period, around 20 million years back, by the end of which all the non-passerine families were established as well as many of the passerines. Poor though the passerine fossil record is, in Miocene/Pliocene deposits fossil remains have been found attributable to modern passerine genera like *Alauda* (the larks), *Sitta* (the nuthatches) and *Emberiza* (the buntings).

   Viewed overall, the extant orders of birds were all in existence during the Tertiary period, as were many of the families of birds of which those orders are composed. Coming one level lower in the taxonomic scale to the genus, it has been calculated that about ten per cent of living non-passerine genera have been recorded from the Tertiary period and a further thirty per cent from the Quaternary. For the passerines, as would be expected, the fossil 'scores' are poorer: less than one per cent of living genera from the Tertiary period, and about ten per cent from the Quaternary.

We want more fossils!

It is often argued that it is the rarity of bird fossils that lies behind the incompleteness and the lack of clarity of our picture of the derivation of birds from reptile ancestry and their subsequent evolution to the dramatic array of species visible today. Certainly avian bones tend to be more fragile than those of mammals and in most cases there are no telltale teeth (which make enduring fossils) to assist our studies. However, that said, bird bones are often larger and stronger than those of fish, amphibians and reptiles, and certainly are more robust than the remains of many invertebrates. We know, too, that under favourable conditions bird fossils can be found in abundance, as at Smoky Hill in Kansas, Rancho La Brea near Los Angeles, the Olduvai Gorge in Tanzania (also famous for hominid and pre-hominid fossils), Aquitaine in France and the London clay of the Isle of Sheppey in Kent, to name a few such localities.

To date, rather fewer than 2000 fossil species of birds have been described, including over 900 extinct fossil species and about the same number of species which are still in existence. It has been powerfully argued that only fifteen research palaeontologists have been involved in the identification of over three quarters of the extinct fossil birds, against the hundreds of researchers involved with fossil reptiles and with mammals. Thus, the argument runs, our lack of knowledge of early forms of birds is not due to the alleged shortage of fossils but more to the lack of dedicated and ornithologically-orientated research workers. If this, as seems likely, is the case, then in years to come, given that sufficient stimulus and incentives have been provided, we can look forward to the discovery of some of the painfully conspicuous 'missing links'. This will help to make our knowledge of the diary of the origins of birds much fuller, more detailed and more meaningful – and even more fascinating.

2

The Specialities of Birds

In most people's minds the words 'flight' and 'birds' are scarcely separable – even synonymous – to such a degree that we tend to forget that other groups of animals have broadly similar powers. Indeed, even the term 'masters of the air', though inevitably applied to birds, fails to take account of the vast range of flight adaptations and the phenomenal efficiency of the flight of a truly vast array of insects.

Flying reptiles

Many millions of years ago, in Jurassic times geologically and probably at about much the same period as the earliest birds were appearing, one group of reptiles, the pterosaurs (often popularly known as pterodactyls), developed powers of flight – though whether this flight was flapping (as in the birds and bats) or a mixture of gliding and soaring is still a matter of dispute. In fact the huge span of the leathery wings of some pterosaurs and the small size of the breast muscles powering them strongly indicate that gliding was their major use.

'Pteranodon'

The pterosaurs had a number of bird-like features – lightweight long bones and skulls, for example – but possessed long tails. Flight was carried out by means of a leathery membrane of skin, supported for a short way by the fore-arm, but over most of its length by a greatly extended fourth digit. The first three digits remained as short claws, the fifth – the little finger – was lost. Amongst the biggest of the pterosaurs was *Pteranodon*, some species of which had an enormous 8m (26ft) wingspan.

How bats fly

More recently, one branch of the mammals, the bats, has also adopted flight, more skilfully than the pterosaur reptiles and without question a well-controlled flapping movement rather than elaboration on an ability to glide. Apart from being able to fly, the bats have many of the general, and basically rather primitive, features of the insect-eating mammals (shrews, hedgehogs and the like) of the order *Insectivora*. As in the pterosaurs, the bats' arms and hands are greatly modified to support a leathery wing of skin which, though effective as a flying surface, is extremely vulnerable to accidental damage – the more so in collisions (for example, with wires or trees) because bats are primarily nocturnal and rely on an echo-sounding (or sonar) tactic to locate and identify obstacles as they fly.

Bat

Bats differ from pterosaurs in that much of the patagium (flap of skin) is supported by all four finger digits, each of which is greatly elongated though remaining slender (and thus fragile) to minimize their weight. The hooked thumb remains free for clambering about on rocks or in trees. Unlike the pterosaurs, but like the birds, the bats possess a sternum (breastbone) like a 'keel' for the attachment of the flight muscles. Unlike those of the birds, the bats' clavicle and scapula (shoulder bones) are stout, and they and the sternum are fused into a shoulder girdle that, with the ribs, takes the strains of flight. The bats' rib cage is also unlike that of the birds in that it is not much compressed by the action of flight, and the process of respiration (breathing) is effected by a moveable diaphragm inflating and deflating the lungs (see Chapter 3).

Insect flight

The number of known and described insect species, fossil and present-day, is steadily heading towards the one million mark (there are, for example, almost a quarter of a million beetles – order Coleoptera) and most of these insects are not confined to the ground but can also fly. Thus there are almost one hundred times as many insects as there are birds, and the benefits that wings confer when it comes to dispersal, finding a mate, seeking food and escaping enemies are just as potent.

Feeding moth

In consequence, an account of the techniques and adaptations concerned with insect flight would comfortably overfill an encyclopaedia, so many and varied are they. Suffice it to say that in the world of small-sized, invertebrate animals – the insects have an exo-skeleton (hard external skeleton) and no backbone – it is the insects that rule the air; while it really is true to say that (despite the pterosaurs and the bats – and various 'flying' snakes, lizards, squirrels, lemurs, etc. – which glide on flaps of skin) among the larger, warm-blooded, vertebrate animals – that is, those with an internal bony skeleton and a backbone – the birds *are* the masters.

Feather power

This mastery of the air arises from the one feature of birds that is both obvious and genuinely unique: their covering of feathers. No other animal has feathers, nor is there any bird – short of a diseased one – that does not possess a feather covering. Feathers are made of a tough protein called keratin, which in the reptiles – and indeed on the tarsus (shin) of a bird – forms horny scales. It seems logical to suppose that feathers evolved from reptilian scales, possibly initially to serve as insulation for primitive warm-blooded forms, but as yet no intermediate stage between the horny scale and the fully developed feather has been found among fossil remains. It remains puzzling that, although present-day birds possess both horny scales and an abundance and variety of feathers, again no intermediate forms occur.

Feathers have various uses. The wing feathers both provide lift, keeping the bird airborne, and power the flight by their propulsive force: the ways in which this is achieved so much more effectively than in the fixed-wing aircraft designed and built by man are explored more fully in Chapter 3. The tail feathers, also usually large but particularly long and strong in the more manoeuvrable of birds, provide stability in the air and assist the wings with steering and braking for a landing.

The smooth, almost hard-looking outline of most birds is due to the way in which the body feathers are constructed and arranged to provide extremely efficient streamlining. Beneath this sleek exterior, which is usually windproof and often waterproof, lie the insulating downy feathers keeping the bird's body temperature at a level normally higher than that of most mammals.

Feathers as communicators

Feathers also provide birds with one of their most powerful means of communication other than by calls or song. This communication may be either positive of negative. Perhaps the best example of negative communication is the mottled patterning, often called camouflage (or 'cryptic'), of the plumage of many female birds, needing to sit, well-concealed, on their eggs for many days. Inexperienced, freshly-fledged young, too, are generally drably and spottily plumaged, conferring both the safety benefits of camouflage and preventing them evoking the territorial wrath of their elders (see Chapter 5).

On the positive side is the use of the huge variety of feather patterning and coloration. Feather colours are obtained both from pigmentation and from the optical effects resulting from light striking the feather surfaces. In many species the major uses of the males' bright plumage in the breeding-season (called the 'nuptial' plumage in old bird books relating its use to human wedding finery) lie in attracting and retaining a mate and communicating to others, by a combination of posture and colour, the possession of territory and the intention to defend it (see Chapter 5).

Rather surprisingly, the actual number of feathers on a bird varies considerably; not just, as might be expected, between different species or between adult and young, but also between individuals of the same age and species. There is a general correlation between body size and feather number, however, ranging between under 1000 in some small hummingbirds, through 2000 or 3000 in many finches and buntings, to 25,000 or more in the Bewick's Swan.

One further feature of feathers that deserves mention is their comparative weight for the various tasks that they perform. Individually they may be proverbially 'light as a feather' but collectively, so important are they (and so lightweight for flight are the various other components of the bird's anatomy), that they form a substantial part of the bird's total weight. One Bald Eagle examined in America had a total body weight of 4082 grams, of which 677 grams was composed of feathers (almost seventeen per cent), while the skeleton weighed only 272 grams (about seven per cent).

Among feathers, both modern and ancient, several recognizable types occur. Outwardly the most obvious are the 'varied' feathers – in a sense looking like the vanes of a windmill, with a central shaft flanked on either side by a flat surface. Some of these – notably the flight feathers (the primaries) in the outer half of the wing – are both strong and flexible, qualities particularly evident in larger birds but just as true in smaller ones. This flexibility comes not just from the nature of the protein keratin of which feathers are made, but also from the intricately detailed structure of the feather itself.

The structure of a feather

A typical vaned feather has a long, strong, central shaft (radius) which at its base (where it is embedded in the skin) is called a quill. It is this portion of the primary feathers of large birds like swans that was cut to the shape of a nib to produce the quill pens of old. On either side of the shaft are the vanes, superficially flat and smooth. Examine them, though, through a magnifying glass, and the complexity of feather structure is revealed. Lying at an angle to the central shaft, close-packed and parallel to one another, are the barbs, plainly visible to the naked eye. These are held – and must be so held for effective flight – in such close formation by a series of hooked barbules. These, too, are a series of parallel filaments branching off the barb in the same way as the barb branches off the radius, but the forward-pointing barbules are equipped with many tiny hooks, which latch on to the rearward-pointing barbule of the barb in front. The backward-pointing barbules lack hooks but have a rolled-over curved edge on to which the hooks from the forward-pointing barbules lock very firmly indeed.

Flight feather

On some larger birds like herons, cranes and swans, the barbs of the biggest flight feathers may have several hundred barbules on each side, amounting to a total of more than one million barbules on the entire feather. When a preening bird runs a feather through its beak, it is these hooks that it is re-arranging in position. Should a bird be involved in an accidental collision with some twigs and disrupt the smooth, strong arrangement, the feathers are merely ruffled and can quickly be preened back to full efficiency.

Types of feather

Many of the vaned feathers that cover the bulk of the body – called 'contour feathers', which implies their importance to streamlining – have downy bases, and some carry a small ancillary downy feather, called an 'aftershaft', attached at the quill. These downy feathers, though basically similar in structure, are not held close-knit by barbules and tend to be much fluffier and thus far better at providing an insulating layer of trapped air close to the bird's skin – in the same way that thermal underclothing does for us. They are augmented in this function by semiplumes, downy feathers with a central radius but whose barbules lack hooks.

Even more loosely constructed are the true down feathers. These, particularly obvious as the lining of ducks' nests, are among the best of insulating layers known, superior to the great majority of man-made synthetic fibre alternatives, which is why polar explorers still rely on down to fill their sleeping bags and parkas. Eider down is familiar to all as the original filling, still commercially 'harvested' by Icelandic farmers, of an 'eiderdown' bed covering; and, interestingly, the increasingly popular continental quilt or duvet derives its name from the French name (*duvet*) for the Eider Duck!

Down

The remaining two feather types are more specialized. One, the filoplume, is a bristle-like feather with a small tuft of down at its tip: it is thought to be a degenerate type, and is best seen on a freshly plucked chicken, which seems to be sparsely covered in these insignificant hair-like structures. They may also be the origin of the bristles around the mouths of flycatchers, swifts and nightjars – called rictal bristles – and as such fulfil an important role in increasing the insect-catching capability of the already widely gaping mouth.

Contour feather

The other remaining feather type is powder down, yellowish down-like feathers growing in clumps on the breast and flanks, particularly of members of the heron family. Unlike other feathers, they grow continuously and do not moult out, and the barb tips break down to produce a supply of fine, water-repellent powder. Birds like herons, that lack the oil-producing preen gland, tend to be well-supplied with powder down and to use it as a waterproofing and conditioning agent, as we would use a special talcum powder.

Feather growth

Most feathers, in contrast, do not grow continuously, and do wear out with time and continuous usage. Feathers are produced in cells in the skin, in much the same way as human hairs. These cells are usually arranged not all over the bird's body but in special tracts, best seen in a nestling song bird just a few days old. Then they appear as dark streaks (dark because of the blood still surrounding the developing feather within its sheath), one usually covering the crown and running centrally down the back, with branches extending out along and above and below the leading edges of the wings, and another starting on the throat but dividing into two tracts running down either side of the breast and belly to rejoin around the anus.

Flight and tail feathers, though similarly formed, arise in their serial places along the wing trailing edge and around the stubby, fleshy tail. The feather grows from its base and receives nutrients via a blood supply entering through a hole in the base of the quill. Once the feather is complete, this blood supply ceases and the feather becomes 'dead', simply implanted in the skin and moved by muscles within the skin, not attached to itself.

The importance of feather maintenance

To maintain its feathers in prime condition is one of the more important aspects of a bird's life, one that demands continued attention if the powers of flight or – just as vital – the waterproofing or insulation properties are to remain effective. This is why so many birds seem to the human observer to spend an inordinate amount of time preening.

The preening process involves running the feathers through the beak to ensure that the barbule hooks are all properly engaged, and in addition adding powder down or, more commonly, oil from the preen gland to enhance feather condition. The preen gland is situated just above the tail, and an oily substance from it is normally applied by rubbing the head and beak over the gland and then across areas of feathers to spread the oil about. Dust-bathing, so familiar in small garden birds like the House Sparrow, also helps, as does the habit of many birds of bathing even in near-freezing weather conditions: this further underlines the importance of good feather maintenance.

Some birds have life styles that lead them into messier conditions than most – the Kingfisher in summer, for example, waddling up its tunnel to a nest chamber lined with foul-smelling remnants of fish and the excrement of its young. There is no way that the adult Kingfisher can avoid soiling its spectacularly colourful plumage, so on emerging from the hole after a feeding visit, the Kingfisher commonly plops immediately down into the stream, splashing vigorously to clean itself.

It is perhaps for the same reason – having fish as its major prey item – that the Heron has its liberal supply of powder down. Herons, too, have an unusual claw adaptation (shared with the Nightjar) which is of great use in cleaning fish scales from the feathers: the underside of the long claw of the middle toe is serrated (pectinate) and operates rather like a comb.

Feather replacement

In all birds the feathers (apart from powder down) eventually become worn and must be replaced. This process (moulting) is for most birds an annual event. For some smaller birds, however, like the Willow Warbler, it occurs twice annually; while for some large ones, like the Golden Eagle and the Gannet, it may be more gradual, with not all feathers shed each year.

The normal pattern of events (sometimes modified to suit special circumstances, as in the breeding Sparrowhawk – see Chapter 5) is that at the close of the breeding season the adult birds will lose, and replace, all of their feathers in an orderly sequence. For resident species this process may occupy two months or more, while some migrants, needing fresh feathers for their long journey but under pressure also to raise two broods *and* to depart southwards before their food supply runs out, complete it in little over a month. Moult progress in late summer and autumn is typified – in its orderly progress, the time it takes, and in its ease of observation to the birdwatcher – by the changing of the wing flight feathers: the primaries (outer section) and secondaries (the inner part of the wing).

Moult commences with the shedding of the innermost primary at the angle on the trailing edge of the wing. Other feathers, as the moult moves steadily outwards, soon follow, leaving a conspicuous gap – this is perhaps most readily seen in birds like the Rooks and the Black-headed Gull. After three or four primaries have been shed, the outermost secondary falls, followed by others in sequence, moving inwards towards the body, and the replacement feathers – beginning with the new innermost primary – begin to appear. As they break through the skin, these are dark quills and not readily visible, but soon the shaft and vanes emerge from the quill sheath and steadily lengthen. Thus the central 'gap-toothed' appearance soon changes to two notches in the trailing edge of the wing, indicating the progress of moult, one moving outwards to the wingtip, the other inwards towards the body.

At much the same time the body feathers are serially shed and replaced, finishing off with those on the head. In most cases, the juvenile birds that abound in late summer moult only their body feathers, not their wings and tail which have hardly had time to wear out to any degree. The wear argument logically applies also to the body feathers, but here the other uses of feathers, particularly in display, dominate the process.

The juvenile Blackbird, for example, leaves the nest with a speckled brown plumage, ideal for camouflage, be it male or female. During the winter and early spring it will need to be able to play a full role in the reproductive life of the local Blackbird community, which a neutral camouflage plumage would not allow. Thus, in the autumn moult, the replacement body feathers on the juvenile Blackbird are jet black in the case of males, rich uniform brown in the case of females, and once this moult is complete the two sexes can occupy their proper place in Blackbird society.

Juvenile Robin

The 'teenage' transition period is more easily seen in young Robins, when the buff-spotted, drab-brown, juvenile breast plumage is replaced at moult by at first a spotty scattering of red feathers, then an almost-red breast, before the ultimate full red gorget is achieved and the Robin can display to its rivals – rivals of its own age as well as older birds, perhaps including its parents.

The mystery of migration

Though like flight, migration is far from being a uniquely avian feature, it is another field in which birds excel. Marvellous and intriguing as the migration of eels to and from the Sargasso Sea and British streams undoubtedly is, and phenomenal though the northward push each spring of the Painted Lady butterfly may seem for an insect so small and with such erratic flight, among birds the development of migratory ability reaches its unquestioned peak.

The lives of a great many birds are based on an annual cycle, or rhythm, although there are some exceptions, particularly among tropical sea birds. This annual rhythm may give rise to several sorts of migration: these include local movements, perhaps to lower altitudes in winter; dispersals – particularly in the case of those pelagic sea birds coming ashore annually to the same colony to breed; and what is regarded as 'typical' migration, often on a roughly north–south axis.

Many kinds of birds are described as 'resident' or 'sedentary' in bird books because they are rarely known to move very far from where they were hatched, but every year in some places these birds do move about locally in a way that can be described as orderly and thus is a form of migration. It can be as simple as the Yellowhammer's desertion of its hedgerow territory in winter and joining with other finches and buntings in roaming nearby stubble fields, as a flock, until the following spring when it returns to its old haunts. The movement of a pair of Dippers from an upland stream to a position lower down because much of their strip of territory is frozen, or flowing but beneath a layer of ice and snow, also qualifies as migration. Meadow Pipits, too, so numerous and a typical sight on summer moorland, descend to lower altitudes, often also further south, to overwinter on arable farmland and coastal marshes.

Within any one species there is considerable scope for variation since some individuals of normally resident species may carry out true migrations. The Starling is a case in point: most British-breeding Starlings are resident and do not move more than locally, whereas those just across the Channel on the Continent migrate westwards as a routine in autumn to overwinter in Britain.

Sea-bird migration

The movements of many sea birds are governed by the necessity of breeding during the summer season, rather than by any need to move, for example, south in winter. Outside the breeding season they may disperse for hundreds, even thousands, of kilometres from their breeding haunts. It is not just a matter of their having the whole ocean to feed in, but more that they have only a limited number of suitably safe sites at which they can nest.

It used to be thought that dispersal after breeding of birds like Gannets, Kittiwakes and the auk family (Puffin, Guillemot and Razorbill) was as much as anything governed by the proximity of the shore and the depth of the waters in otherwise fish-rich seas. However, detailed analyses of the recoveries of ringed birds indicate that particular colonies, or groups of colonies, each have commonly-used wintering areas, not all governed by a routine autumn movement in a single compass direction but some north, some south, some east and some west. Even young birds may have different wintering ranges from adults in the same colonies.

Population fluctuation

Some birds – and it seems that the number of species involved is rather larger than at first thought – undergo more or less regular changes in population levels. When a peak of population is reached, it very often means that local food sources are put under intolerable pressure, and this threat of starvation provokes a mass movement (in Europe usually westwards or south-westwards) that certainly qualifies as a sort of migration, usually called an 'irruption'. Most of these mass movements seem to occur at five- to fifteen-year intervals, commonly about every decade.

In Britain, irruptive movements of the Crossbill from Europe follow this pattern, resulting in mass arrivals every few years. Often enough, the irruption is so large that numbers of Crossbills stay on and breed, on occasion seeming to establish new colonies or outposts for their species, as is the case with the otherwise isolated colony of these birds in Norfolk.

The Collared Dove explosion

Thus in a way, range extension can also loosely fit under the heading of migration. By far the best example of this – likely to be the best ever – is also a recent one. The Collared Dove, half a century ago, was a little-known distant relative of the Turtle Dove, resident in North Africa and Asia as near to Europe as Turkey. Then, quite suddenly, this previously static species started a phenomenal westward spread across

Europe. Quite what triggered the change is not fully understood, but it seems most likely to be genetic in origin. Certainly the spread broke all the 'rules', particularly the popular 'nature abhors a vacuum'.

It is normally considered that, in most cases, all the available 'niches' – food, nest sites, habitats – in an ecosystem are filled, and that any newcomer to that system can only gain a foothold at the expense of one or more of the original occupants. Thus when the Collared Dove expanded west, it was assumed that some other species would suffer, the Turtle Dove being the most likely candidate. But this did not happen: the Collared Dove seems to have exploited two habitats – urban areas on the one hand and cereal farmland (or poultry farms where large quantities of cereals are used as feed) on the other – displacing nothing detectable in the process.

In 1955 and 1956 the first two or three pairs of Collared Doves had penetrated west as far as England, where they nested, shrouded in secrecy and extreme excitement. Within a decade they had reached pest status in parts of Eastern England, parasitizing poultry farms and living and breeding year-round in and around grain-storage silos. Within two decades, they were breeding over all of Britain and Ireland, and their numbers had risen to perhaps 50,000 pairs, on a par with such species as Rock Pipit, Great Spotted Woodpecker, and perhaps even Turtle Dove.

Typical migrants

However, to return to more normal migrations: most of the summer-visiting birds to Britain and Ireland, and nearly all of the winter visitors, are typical migrants. This implies that they have two distinct ranges though in some cases these ranges may to some degree overlap, as is the case with the Chiff-chaff. Between these two ranges the migrants make their journey each autumn and spring – and while on that journey they are said to be 'on passage'.

Clearly there must be some very positive reasons for such complex migrations to have evolved. The most obvious one is that creatures like birds, endowed with extremely well-developed powers of flight – and, it must be added, obviously also of navigation – are able to exploit distant areas which, while rich in food during the summer months, are impossibly cold and hostile during the winter. The actual degree of 'impossibly cold' naturally varies with the species of bird involved.

Thus some species, like the many warblers breeding in Britain and Ireland and other summer visitors, move from overwintering areas in the tropics (where there are no winter/summer seasonal changes) to

exploit our temperate climate and a summer-long richness of insect life that allows them to raise two or three broods of young during their visit. Others – like many of the ducks, geese and waders overwintering in the temperate parts of Western Europe, particularly the warmer Atlantic seaboard hasten even further north in summer to take advantage of the brief Arctic summer. They must time their arrival with some precision, arriving as the snow and ice retreat, but although the summer is brief and climatically treacherous, the crop of insects and their larvae waiting to be harvested by the summer visitors is enormous in most years and raising a single brood may not be difficult if the timing is right. Were it not a successful strategy – particularly for the larger, longer-lived birds tending to exploit it – evolution would surely have eliminated it from use.

The effect of weather patterns

An inspection of the isotherm maps for the whole of Europe and Asia shows why migration is by no means solely on a north–south axis to exploit summer richness. Looking at midwinter temperatures, the lowest (at −50°C/−60°F) are to be found in Siberia, but it is also evident that much of Northern Eurasia is completely inhospitable in midwinter except to a small handful of extremely specialized birds like the Ptarmigan. Birds retreating from this cold region may well move west–south-west, following the temperature gradient to the milder winters of coastal Europe, which derives benefit from the oceanic currents of the Atlantic, like the Gulf Stream, bringing relatively warm waters from the tropics quite far north.

The existence of the Himalayas along the southern edge of the Eurasian land mass may be another incentive for a westward movement, particularly for small birds, but there are striking exceptions to this broad rule as in the case of the Bar-headed Goose. This species provides one of the most striking examples of the physique necessary for migrant birds, for it routinely overflies the Himalayas, occasionally to be seen in the thin, oxygen-deficient air at heights exceeding that of Mount Everest.

A migration crossroads

Britain and Ireland lie at a form of migration crossroads, well-situated for birdwatchers with an interest in migration. In European terms Britain and Ireland are relatively mild 'offshore islands' to a continental land mass that has much colder winters; thus they serve as a refuge for many birds of all sorts escaping this winter cold. There is a steady stream of migrants, ranging in size from Wheatears to waders and geese, passing south in autumn, north in spring, from and to Iceland and Greenland. Some pass on, like the Greenland Wheatear heading for tropical Africa; others, like the Barnacle Goose, stay for the winter.

Another stream leaves the Arctic tundra via Scandinavia, and returns that way in spring. Once again, some species stay with us, like many of the waders, while others, like the terns, move on further south. The picture is complicated by the fact that while some of the waders may stay in Britain and Ireland through the winter, others of the same species travel further south, even much further south, as far as Southern Africa. The Knot is a case in point.

To these movements can be added the departures from Britain and Ireland of the summer visitors like the Swifts, Swallows, warblers and all the others that enhance our summer days, and the arrivals of the multitude of winter visitors (Redwings, Fieldfares, Starlings, and so on) displaced from Central and Northern Europe by the early advent of winter. Further complexity arises from the variability both in timing and in the number of birds involved, both of which are influenced to a large degree by how hard a winter it is and by the location and timing of its impact.

Nor are these once-and-for-all movements, for should the weather worsen, or improve, during the winter, additional migratory traffic will be generated. Often this is best to be seen in flocking birds that move in daylight – characteristic examples of birds that carry out such 'weather movements' are Lapwings, Skylarks and Woodpigeons – and westward-moving flocks of any of these species should warn the alert birdwatcher to turn up the central-heating thermostat or get in a supply of logs!

The terns

The terns, aptly given the popular name 'sea swallows', are perhaps the most graceful and elegant of our sea birds. Silver-grey and white, with darker wingtips and black cap, and long swallow-like tail streamers, they are smaller and much slimmer than any of the gulls. All are migrants, travelling to fish in the oceans of the southern hemisphere during the winter, returning to our coasts to breed in summer, and they offer some of the most striking examples of long-range migration available among our birds.

The Arctic Tern probably sees more hours of daylight each year than any other creature. Arctic Terns breed in Northern Britain, and further north up into the Arctic Circle where the summer is virtually nightless. Having raised their young on the short-lived summer abundance of insects and fish, they migrate southwards, crossing the Equator to spend our winter in the Antarctic Ocean. Here again they have the benefit of almost perpetual daylight, and enjoy an immensely rich food supply of small fish and plankton. There is even one recovery of a ringed bird aboard a whaling vessel just off the pack ice.

Arctic Tern

The oldest Arctic Tern that we know of was a ringed bird that lived for twenty-six years. Travelling almost from pole to pole twice each year, the distance it covered during its lifetime is unthinkably high: certainly several million kilo-metres. A ringed Common Tern, a close relative, has been found in Australia, but despite this propensity for long-distance travel terns can often be seen feeding close inshore near our coastal holiday resorts, either because the resorts are reasonably close to their usually rather secluded breeding colonies, or in spring or late summer (high season for the holiday trade is August, which is the time that terns start to think of heading south again) when they are on passage. In either case, terns spend much of their time fishing close inshore, flickering along lazily in the air a few metres above the waves before suddenly turning and plunging headlong into the sea. Often such dives result in an audible 'plop' and a considerable splash, but the bird penetrates only a few centimetres, rather than submerging deeply, in its quest for small fish or shrimps.

The perils of migration

So the power of migration offers to birds a number of advantages, particularly those associated with the seasonal colonization of a large and – in food terms – profitable area of the earth's surface not available year-round. What, though, are the disadvantages of migration, the hazards of the immense journeys that may be involved? Clearly predators will be waiting for the migrant hordes to pass, perhaps too intent on the stresses of the journey, or considering themselves relatively safe as just one of a flock, to be properly individually alert to danger.

Sadly, even today, man is one of the major killers: in southern France and Spain, pigeons and doves are slaughtered in thousands each autumn; and it is estimated that further east in the Mediterranean millions of birds perish each year at the hands of the bird-limers, who now use modern adhesives to coat perching twigs in place of the old-fashioned sticky lime plaster. The birds are quickly trapped by feet or feather but are left for hours in distress before being removed and killed. This so-called hunting is rarely to satisfy local food shortages, but far more often the warblers and nightingales are destined for the lucrative delicatessen market of supposedly civilized countries in Northern Europe, Britain included.

Other more natural predators include two species of falcon – Eleanora's Falcon in the Mediterranean and the Sooty Falcon further south – which have adapted to the abundance of autumn migrants to feed their young. In autumn the numbers of migrants are greatly swollen by the young produced during the summer, and in delaying their breeding season, laying in July and August, these falcons have evolved a strategy by which the time when the young are at their most demanding coincides with the peak of food abundance.

Weather difficulties

Weather, too, must often pose problems, particularly as the further north from the equator you move, the more variable and the less predictable the weather becomes. Storms can literally knock small birds from the air, strong winds can drift migrants hundreds of kilometres off course, and fog, thick cloud or heavy rain can confuse their otherwise brilliantly accurate navigation. Headwinds can obviously hasten exhaustion – and, just as in a motor vehicle, also increase fuel consumption – which can easily prove fatal particularly if a desert – many of our summer visitors must overfly the Sahara – or sea crossing is involved.

For most land birds, the Mediterranean Sea is the major water hazard between Europe and Africa, and it is noticeable that many migrants – most conspicuous among them the soaring birds like the raptors, cranes and storks – opt for the shortest of sea crossings at the Straits of Gibraltar or the Bosporus.

But those migrants whose summering areas lie to the north-west of Britain needs must accomplish a sea crossing to Greenland or Iceland, a journey over the notoriously stormy waters or the North Atlantic of around 1000km (620 miles). Many waders seem to take the route of travelling overland to Northern Scandinavia, then heading west, but most geese are thought to tackle the journey direct.

Geese tend to travel in groups of families and normally fly in some form of staggered 'V' formation. In this formation older, experienced and more powerful birds (usually females) take turns in leading and in consequence navigating. It is also suggested by aerodynamics experts that the birds in the arms of the 'V' each derive some benefit, in the form of additional 'lift', from the turbulence created by the beating wings of the birds in front. In this way the group has the best chance of both remaining on course and of conserving energy on a long and hazardous journey. How much more remarkable, then, seems the trip that the Greenland race of the Wheatear, smaller than a Song Thrush and, so far as is known, without the aid of a social structure like that found in a skein of geese, also carries out twice each year over the same route!

Experts in navigation

Behind such migratory feats lies the ever-present marvel of the birds' abilities to navigate. It is more than a little sobering to think that in a Chiff-chaff, weighing about 7 grams in total, and with a head little bigger than the tip-most joint of a human little finger, is centred a navigational computing system capable of guiding the bird on its return – at *each* end of its migration – not only to the same country, but to the same county – or its equivalent – and even to the same wood, copse or thicket when it returns the following season. Perhaps we should consider such skills when highlighting our own space-age technological marvels, especially those based on microchips!

To navigate with such precision demands an ability to know where you are at any given time, and to recognize when you have reached your destination. For mankind, such navigation has, since the invention of the chronometer for use with the sextant to plot accurately the angle of the sun at midday, required accurate information of the time, and knowledge of disruptive forces, like crosswinds, is essential. It is possible that many birds know and recognize their neighbourhood and the surrounding countryside from experience, much as we do. Certainly, although many adult migrants return to the same location year after year, most young birds do not, but only return to the same part of the country, which demands much less precision.

Diurnal (daytime) migrants may also learn the route of their migration, following their 'elders and betters' who already know the way, perhaps along coasts or the lines of rivers or hills. However, this cannot explain how young Cuckoos reach their wintering grounds in Africa safely, having left Europe at least a month after all the knowledgeable adults have departed. Nor can such visual signals help that great majority of small birds like the warblers and thrushes, much of whose migration is carried out after dark.

The amazing case of the Manx Shearwater

Navigational accuracy over an annual route – or at least a route which is ancestrally known – is one thing, and amazing enough, but a 'homing ability', the ability to be able to get back no matter where you are, is even more remarkable. By far the most striking story is of a Manx Shearwater. Manx Shearwaters are sea birds and, as their name suggests, fly low, often touching the waves with one wingtip as they bank and turn. The wings are long and narrow and held stiff, slightly bowed downwards. Only in very still air do they flap; otherwise, Shearwaters cut at speed across the ocean air currents, gaining lift even off the waves, and Welsh birds may regularly fish for food as far away from home as the Bay of Biscay, so fast and energy-saving is their flight.

Shearwaters nest underground, mostly on remote and usually uninhabited islands, and they visit their breeding areas only at night. By day, walking the cliff top, there would be no reason to suspect that a colony existed in the 'rabbit burrows' all around; but at night the adults' eerie caterwauling as they fly overhead with a rush of air like a wartime shell, gives the game away. The adults change over incubation duty, or feed their solitary chick, covered in great masses of fluffy

grey down, at night to escape the savage predation that the Great-backed Gull can wreak as the clumsy Shearwaters struggle towards their burrows. The sitting bird may have been waiting a few days for its mate to return from a fishing trip, and responds eagerly to the crowing, cooing call as it passes overhead. In this way, even in the dark, the right nest is quickly located.

Perhaps the bird navigation feat of all time was performed in a homing experiment by one such Manx Shearwater, ring number AX6587, from the breeding colony on Skokholm Bird Observatory off the south-west tip of Wales. AX6587 was taken off her nest, placed in a dark but comfortable transit box, flown by commercial airliner to Boston, USA, almost 5000km (3100 miles) away and far from any normal Shearwater haunts. There she was released and just twelve and a half days later she had safely returned to her nesting burrow on the island, beating the airmail letter from America, giving details of the date and time of her release, by a short head!

How birds navigate

It is not too difficult to imagine that birds are endowed with a much more precise sense of timing than us – and even human timing, when practised and then put to the test, is better than we often imagine – and with a much better sense of direction. We know from experiments with caged nocturnal migrants placed in a planetarium that many of them have an innate 'basic' migration direction, and that this can be changed – to the correct and expected degree – by moving the star patterns on the artificial planetarium sky. Similarly, day migrants offered a sight of the sun from their cage, but reflected in a mirror, will change the direction in which they try to fly off by the appropriate correction factor. Most can apparently correct for crosswind drift to some degree, and if they have been displaced – actually on migration, or by being transported artificially off-course during experiments – they can make a very good attempt at adjusting their bearings to reach their original destination.

Experimentally, adult Starlings have been shown to be far better at this re-orientation than juveniles. And, too, most day or night migrants seem able to cope with a light overcast, but not with heavy cloud or rain, which usually causes them to get lost and to make landfall at the earliest opportunity. It is clear that migrant birds have an innate directional sense, and that they have an inbuilt 'knowledge' of sun location and time of day, or alternatively of star patterns and time.

It has been suggested that other factors may play a part in birds' navigation too. One such theory is the earth's magnetic field (though experiments on birds with magnets attached to alter this field have been inconclusive); another their sense of smell. So far as we can discover, most birds have the appropriate sensory nerves, and a well-developed olfactory part of the brain, to smell effectively, but few seem to use it on a day-to-day basis. Even humans, with their very poor sense of smell, can detect differences as they travel, each area having some characteristic aroma, perhaps based on soil, or plants, or even on foodstuffs (like garlic and olives). Perhaps, it is argued, the birds may do likewise.

Just how do birdwatchers investigate the migrations of birds? Since biblical times we have known about migration as an annual seasonal event. The *Song of Solomon* refers to the phenomenon in the following lines: 'For lo, the winter is past, the rain is over and gone; the flowers appear on the earth; the time of the singing of birds is come; and the voice of the turtle is heard in our land' – the 'turtle' being the Turtle Dove with its purring song and not a reference to the voiceless reptile. Even so, accurate knowledge of bird movements was so scant that only a couple of hundred years ago Swallows and House Martins were thought to overwinter by hibernating in the mud at the bottom of ponds!

The ancients also knew something of birds' powers of navigation, or at least of their 'homing' abilities. As far back as the Punic Wars in 300 BC, marked Swallows were used in the role of carrier pigeons. Adult Swallows were taken from their nestlings and smuggled out of besieged garrisons: they were later released, to 'home' to their nests, with a message attached to their legs giving details of the relief force's progress. Shortly afterwards the results of chariot races in Rome were conveyed to Volterra – about 200km (125 miles) away – quickly and effectively by tying threads of the winner's colours to the Swallows' legs, doubtless allowing those who wished to do so the opportunity of defrauding the bookies of the day!

What we learn from ringing

At the beginning of this century, in both Denmark and Britain, the technique of marking birds with a numbered metal ring fitted neatly to the leg (first used in mediaeval times by falconers) was extended and developed, and since then a host of amateur and professional bird-watchers worldwide has taken part. As a result our understanding of the routes taken, the timings and the destinations of migrants has increased immensely.

Each ring has a serial number stamped on it, individually identifiable just like a car number plate, together with an address for its return if found. The national ringing centre (in Britain, the British Trust for Ornithology at Tring in Hertfordshire) keeps the records of when and where the bird was marked – today all this information is filed on computer – so that should the bird be recovered, the information is readily available to the researcher and ringing details can be sent to the finder. Naturally, not all birds with rings on are found: recovery rates vary from below one per cent for small birds like the Willow Warbler, to about thirty per cent for large, conspicuous ones like swans.

Many birds are marked as nestlings in the nest, which allows great precision in ageing and in identifying the place of origin. The majority, though, are specially caught for ringing by a variety of techniques mostly developed from those used by hunters catching birds for food in the past. These traps range from the simple sieve, propped up over bait by a stick to which a pull-string is attached, to huge walk-in wire-netting funnel traps, with a glass-fronted catching box at the narrow end, called 'Heligoland traps' after the island bird observatory at which they were invented.

Far more portable, and responsible perhaps for at least half the birds ringed in Britain annually (the total is usually between half and three quarters of a million), are mist nets. These nets, normally constructed of man-made fibres, have a texture rather like that of a hair net, and range from a few metres to 20 metres (65ft) in length by 2–3 metres (6.5–10ft) high. Their catching efficiency, set across flightlines and against the background of bushes or trees, is very high because they

Heligoland trap

are fine enough to be invisible to all intents and purposes to the flying bird. So soft and elastic are they that the flying bird is brought gently to rest before dropping into a pocket, unharmed, to await removal by the bird ringer.

Ringing cannot be the only way of studying migration, as many birds do not migrate in a pattern that easily allows it. Daytime migrants, like Swallows, Meadow Pipits and Skylarks, can be observed and counted by watchers at the network of bird observatories across Europe, and by ordinary birdwatchers in the field. But what of the night migrants? Here, technology comes to the birdwatchers' aid.

Radar-tracking migrants

Soon after the invention of radar, scientists were puzzled by echoes or 'blips', resembling those produced by aeroplanes but much slower-moving, that they nicknamed 'angels'. These angels assumed snowstorm-like proportions in spring and autumn, when all seemed to be moving on the same heading: south or south-west in autumn, north or north-east in spring. Eventually angels were identified as flocks of migrant birds, a discovery that opened a new field for students of both day and night migration.

Radar can 'see' further than the human eye in worse visibility and can cover a far greater area in one scan – all great advantages over a single birdwatcher. It has, though, its problems: some birds show echo characteristics that allow them to be identified on radar, but others can only be classified as small, medium or large, and numbers are always difficult to estimate. Nevertheless, to see a time-lapse film of a radar screen, photographed through the night at peak migration times, is a really dramatic means of appreciating just how broad the migration front is and how huge are the numbers of birds involved. Radar also allows easier study of the impact of wind strength and of the influence exerted by a change in weather, as heralded by the migrants meeting oncoming rain clouds.

On a more parochial scale, radar can help by showing local movements, most characteristically of Starlings. The echoes of Starlings leaving their huge communal roosts in the early morning, known as 'ring angels', look just like the concentric ripples that spread out after a pebble has been dropped into the still, smooth water of a pond. The ring angels have been shown to be Starlings leaving in all directions from the roost, in batches but spaced out at regular time intervals.

The thrill of ringing recoveries

Valuable though the routine bulk of ringing recoveries is in aiding our knowledge and interpretation of migration, inevitably it is the spectacular recoveries that catch and hold the eye. The navigational ability of an adult Manx Shearwater has already featured in this account, but the young also deserve mention. The parent Shearwaters feed the single youngster a smelly, oily mixture of fish and plankton which is very nutritious. On this it grows quickly, becoming very fat – and itself nutritious: in Australasia a related species, the 'mutton bird', is still eaten by man.

A couple of weeks before fledging the young bird is far too heavy to fly. Its parents then abandon it and return to sea while it converts its stored fat into muscle and completes its feather growth, eventually slimming and maturing enough to emerge one night from its burrow to embark on its maiden flight, *en route* to wintering grounds off Brazil, where others of its kind congregate annually.

As if this were not far enough, one Manx Shearwater, almost certainly not on a 'routine mission' but far from its normal areas, is on record as one of the most distant of recoveries of a bird ringed in Britain, being recovered on the shores of the Great Australian Bight. Both Common and Arctic Terns have already also been mentioned as reaching South-eastern Australia, almost diametrically opposite (on the globe) their place of birth.

Most striking long-range ringing recoveries tend to feature larger birds. Not only do they usually have the better physique to undertake such long voyages, but also, being bigger and more conspicuous, their chances of being found – or indeed, as many are waders or wildfowl, of being shot for food – are much greater than those of a small bird.

Swallow at nest

That said, there are several recoveries of British-ringed Swifts in Central Africa and many reports of British-breeding Swallows from roosts (during the British winter months) in the Republic of South Africa. Some ringed Spotted Flycatchers, too, have penetrated to the extreme southern hemisphere tip of Africa.

Equally impressive are the occasional arrivals in Britain, and elsewhere in Western Europe, of oriental birds. One of the most dramatic is the Pallas's Warbler, little bigger or heavier than a Goldcrest, which breeds in Southern Siberia and Northern China and winters in South-east Asia. Every few years, usually associated with a massive area of high barometric pressure centred in mid-Europe, several of these tiny birds may reach our shores, perhaps under the influence of easterly winds fetching from as far afield as China.

British migration records

Southernmost Australasian ringing recoveries have already been mentioned, as have the now numerous reports of Manx Shearwaters off the coasts of Brazil and Argentina, where occasional recoveries of both Arctic and Great Skuas have also occurred. Thus it is the northern hemisphere that remains to be highlighted – and what highlights they are!

Starting in the west, the westernmost recovery of a British-ringed bird is of a Mallard, recovered in the prairie provinces of Canada at the foot of the Rockies at longitude 120°W. Only slightly less distant westwards, and considerably further to the north (north of the Arctic Circle) fall the recoveries of a Knot on its Baffin Island breeding grounds, and of both Knot and Turnstone on the northwestern coast of Greenland. In such remote areas, humans are either absent or extremely scarce and widely scattered, so were it not for special scientific expeditions to study these birds on their breeding grounds, reported recoveries of ringed birds would be even fewer.

Knot at nest

    Further south on the west coast of Greenland are some Arctic and Great Skua recoveries, indicating – with those in South America – the huge north–south span of the range of these two species, in this case outside the breeding season. From the north-eastern coast of Greenland, British-ringed migrant Turnstone and Ringed Plovers have been reported from their tundra breeding grounds.

    Looking eastwards from the Greenwich meridian, there are many recoveries from Arctic Russia, and its offshore islands like Spitzbergen and Jan Meyen, of White-fronted Geese, Tufted Duck, Bar-tailed Godwit and Dotterel; and, further to the south, of Wigeon and Snipe, all of these stretching away to 90°E, a flight of some 8000km (4970 miles). The easternmost records of British-ringed birds, though, are quite fantastic: a Ruff, just south of the Arctic Circle and at a longitude of about 130°E (roughly the same easting as Korea) and, as with the westernmost record, again a duck but this time a Pochard, recovered on the shores of the Sea of Okhotsk, almost as far as the Kamchatka Peninsula, at about 150°E.

Still much to learn

Gilbert White, the great Hampshire parson-naturalist, lived at a time when, although migration was receiving considerably more credence than before, many were still doubtful if such journeys were feasible – especially by the more lowly of God's creatures. White himself was clearly in two minds when, writing from Selborne in 1771, he stated: 'We must not, I think, deny migration in general; because migration certainly does subsist in certain places, as my brother in Andalusia has fully informed me. Of the motions of these birds, he has ocular demonstration . . . .'

There is a certain irony in the fact that, over 200 years later with about 150,000 House Martins now ringed, of which about 8000 have been recovered, with all the skills now at our disposal and with extremely good ornithological coverage over the whole of Africa, all we can yet say of the winter range of the House Martin is that our suspicion of its lying somewhere in Africa was borne out by the recovery in Nigeria of the first British-ringed House Martin. Moreover, this occurred only around the time of writing! The contrast is so striking with the case of the House Martin's relative, the Swallow, about whose movements and destinations we know so much.

House Martins

Obviously we have made some giant strides in our knowledge of bird migration since Gilbert White's day, but we still have no comprehensive way of penetrating the mystery of migration. How bird navigation works in so many different circumstances must remain one of the greatest unsolved biological problems. We have a great store of data and many theories, some simple, some complex and each with some experimental evidence behind it, but for a full explanation of the necessary brain structures and just how birds are so good in the accuracy of their time, distance and direction judgements, we must keep waiting.

3 The Framework for Success

The ability to fly, particularly the ability to fly as well and as effectively as the birds do, makes a number of demands on the structure of the flying creature. Some of these are quite predictable – the conversion of the arm and hand into a wing, for example – but others may be less so. To fly as adroitly as do birds, without expending much energy in maintaining what old-fashioned aeroplane pilots called 'trim' (in aeronautical terms keeping the plane on an even keel both fore and aft and from side to side), it is necessary to have as compact a body as possible, with as many of the vital body organs located close to its centre of gravity as is possible. This the birds have accomplished to a considerable degree.

Many birds – for example, the House Sparrow and the Puffin – are compactly built, but others – strikingly, the Flamingo – may not appear to be so. However, a closer inspection of a Flamingo in flight reveals that it, too, is well balanced for this purpose. The body itself, with weighty parts like muscles, the heart and the digestive tract, is clearly compact, and its centre of gravity lies between the wings – the obvious place for maximum flight efficiency. Those parts of the Flamingo that would seem likely to cause problems in maintaining trim are its head and neck and its legs and feet, but not only are these roughly the same in the lengths to which they protrude fore and aft, they also weigh much

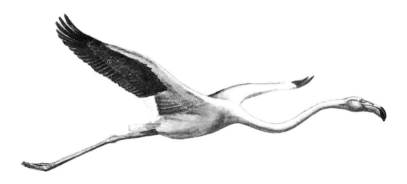

Flamingo

the same, and so are counterbalanced. Thus the Flamingo too conforms to the general rule that the centre of gravity should lie between the wings, as is the case with all flying birds.

Specially adapted bones

Hardly unexpectedly, perhaps the major characteristic of bird bones is their lightness which, though possibly reducing the fossil record, must greatly decrease the energy inputs necessary for flight: it is an obvious adaptation. Though birds may have large bones, they are not massive in weight. Most of the bigger bones are hollow and some have significantly large cavities to hold extensions of the air-sacs of the respiratory system. Occasionally the cavity is crossed by a mesh of bony fibres or, as in the albatrosses, by diagonal bony cross-struts. These bones owe their strength and rigidity to these structures, which are so sophisticated that they are emulated by engineers in modern girder design: the Warren truss, or girder, so familiar in railway bridges is a case in point.

Albatross wing bone interior structure

They are almost unbelievably lighter than a mammal bone of similar size.

The skeleton of the bird is constructed on the same general lines as that of other animals with backbones. It consists of a strong central 'box' of bone, with attachments – the neck and head, the wings, and the legs and feet. The basic structure of the central box – similar in concept to the engineer's box girder – has been illustrated in ancient and modern terms in Chapter 2. At the upper edge, the lumbar or thoracic part of the backbone is relatively short compared with that in most mammals or reptiles. The vertebrae are stout, often almost fused into a solid rod, and are attached at the rear to an elongated and strong pelvic (hip) girdle.

The lower part of the 'girder' is formed by the massive sternum (breast bone), which is keeled to give extra strength to hold the flight muscles. These two large, rigid elements are joined by a series of flattened ribs, which are attached at both ends and form the sides of this rigid box.

For added strength the bird rib possesses a special feature called an 'uncinate process'. This protrudes rearward, like a spur, from the centre of each rib, and overlaps the next rib behind, so greatly fortifying the side walls of the box.

The skeleton as protection

Within this rigid box, the bulk of a bird's vital organs are well protected. Unlike in man, for example, the abdominal area vulnerable to damage in an accident or in a fight with a predator, which lies between the sternum and the pelvic girdle, is minimally small in birds, so long and strong is the sternum. The 'box girder' itself, of course, is subject to evolutionary adaptation. A good example of this may be seen in the Water Rail, among the most secretive and inconspicuous of wetland birds which spends much of its time lurking deep in the reed beds close to the water, advertising its presence only during the breeding season by emitting harsh calls that have been likened to the screams and squeals accompanying the slaughtering of a pig! To slip easily between the densely packed, vertical reed stems, the body skeleton of the Water Rail is compressed from side to side; so, though viewed laterally, it seems almost Moorhen-sized, viewed from the front (or rear) it seems extremely slim for its height.

Additional protection of the body organs is necessary for those birds – often sea birds – that submerge to pursue their prey under water. Many of these, like the terns and a number of the diving ducks, penetrate to depths ranging from only a few centimetres to a few metres. Most of the sea birds and water fowl that swim on the surface and then submerge in search of prey tend to remain under water for less than one minute at a time – and some of this time is spent searching for food or pursuing prey as well as in the actual diving – so clearly they do not reach any great depth.

A characteristic example of such a bird would be the Great Northern Diver which often swims with its head below the water surface, scanning for prey and submerging with hardly a ripple when a fish is spotted. These swimming birds are naturally buoyant, less dense than the water, and take in a breath (making them more buoyant still) before they dive. To save energy they adopt various strategies to overcome this tendency to float. Commonly they compress their feathers to drive out the layer of air trapped beneath them, but some birds have been reported as swallowing stones to reduce their buoyancy as a human diver uses lead weights. It is suggested also that the Cormorant and Shag – so often

Anatomy of a bird's leg

Though the components are broadly the same as in any mammal hind-limb, even the human leg, the proportionate lengths of the various bones in a bird's leg differ. The thigh bone (femur) is normally short and stout and runs almost horizontally forwards from the hip. The true knee of a bird is thus usually concealed in the body feathers, located just below the bird's centre of gravity, and what emerges, looking like a thigh, is in reality the shin (tibio-fibula). It follows that the joint clearly visible in mid-leg, which looks like the knee only fitted the wrong way round, is actually the ankle. The section between the ankle and the clearly recognizable toes is usually slender and covered in scales which differ little from those of reptiles past and present – occasionally, how-ever, it is feathered as in the House Martin and the aptly named Rough-legged Buzzard. Called the tarsus, it is in fact composed of the tarsus and metatarsus fused together into a single long bone. To the end of the tarsus are attached, as a general rule, three forward-pointing toes and one rearward one – ancestrally our 'big toe'. There are never more than four toes.

Thus the bird's leg, with its knee and ankle joints at some distance from the hip and from the point of contact with the ground, and with these two joints (and the elastic ligaments round them) operating in opposite directions, serves both as an extremely efficient shock absorber, taking up the impact of landing, and as an effective 'catapult' launch-ing device, allowing the bird – particularly in an emergency – to spring off directly into flight. Naturally there are heavyweight exceptions – for example, the Mute Swan, with its long, pattering take-off runs. Equally, built as the leg is of three single rigid bones, it is well suited to a wide range of adaptations linked either to locomotion or to feeding.

Familiar extremes in this structural modification include the tiny legs of the Swift, with four *forward*-pointing toes with needle-sharp claws ideal for clinging on to vertical cliffs or brickwork; and the dispropor-tionately minute, bright-red feet of the Kingfisher, so out of scale with its massive head and beak. The Kingfisher's feet are composed of two toes, partly fused together, pointing forwards and a similar rearward-pointing pair. This small foot size comes as a particular surprise in the Kingfisher for, like the similarly puny-footed Bee-eater, it uses its feet to excavate quite a lengthy nesting tunnel in often not very soft soil! These are not the only birds whose structure can present difficulties. At the other end of the scale are wading birds like the Stilt and the Flamingo, with an almost grotesque leg-length that actually causes them problems when they try to stand in a strong wind.

Foot adaptations

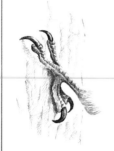

Woodpecker

Owl

Ptarmigan

Robin

Sparrowhawk

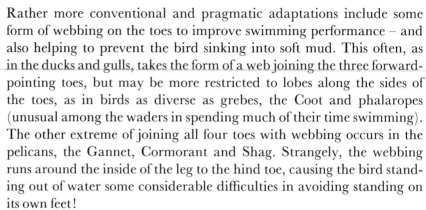

Rather more conventional and pragmatic adaptations include some form of webbing on the toes to improve swimming performance – and also helping to prevent the bird sinking into soft mud. This often, as in the ducks and gulls, takes the form of a web joining the three forward-pointing toes, but may be more restricted to lobes along the sides of the toes, as in birds as diverse as grebes, the Coot and phalaropes (unusual among the waders in spending much of their time swimming). The other extreme of joining all four toes with webbing occurs in the pelicans, the Gannet, Cormorant and Shag. Strangely, the webbing runs around the inside of the leg to the hind toe, causing the bird standing out of water some considerable difficulties in avoiding standing on its own feet!

As powerful propulsive mechanisms, both above and below water, foot webs are often accompanied by leg adaptations – and indeed by an elongation and streamlining of the 'body box'. In many ducks, auks, divers and grebes the legs are relatively short and stout, well muscled, and often set back on the body towards the tail. Though increasing swimming efficiency, this location does so only at the cost of on-land walking capability: the diver family are often called 'loons' – not for their maniacal laughing calls but probably from the Icelandic *lomr*, meaning 'lame' or 'clumsy'.

If webbed feet also offer support on soft mud, so too the long, spidery toes of many marsh and shore wading birds also serve quite adequately to propel a swimmer: the Moorhen is the obvious example. The long-toed birds are often very long-legged too (the Herons, egrets, spoonbills) or at least have medium to long legs, as in the waders, crakes and rails. The Water Rail offers excellent examples of how effective a long-toed foot can be in supporting its owner on both mud and floating vegetation, but even it does not approach the skills of the jacanas, the appropriately-named 'lily-trotters' of the tropics and sub-tropics, that walk with ease from one floating water-lily leaf to the next, spreading their weight on toes spanning more than 10cm (4ins).

The talons of the eagles, hawks, falcons, owls and their relatives are discussed at greater length in Chapter 4. As well as being long in the leg, as has already been mentioned, birds of prey – unlike most birds – have toes which are roughly equal in length, each tipped with a fearsomely sharp claw that not only grasps the prey but usually also deals the death blow. To maximize their catching area, just before the moment of impact the feet are held, outstretched, with the four toes at right angles to each other in the form of a cross. Although many birds of prey take a great deal of carrion as food at times, it is interesting

Gannet

Swift

Coot

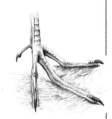

Wader

Duck

that the vultures, which seem rarely if ever actually to kill their prey but always scavenge, though possessed of an eagle-like powerful tearing beak, have relatively weak feet with shortish toes and small, blunt claws rather than talons.

Also adapted to gripping are the toes of the tree-climbing birds. Many of these are in the woodpecker family which have strong legs with robust toes, each armed with a sharply hooked claw, often able to secure a grip even on smooth, hard bark like that of a beech tree. Unusually, woodpecker toes are set two forwards, two back, to offer better grip on a vertical surface. Woodpeckers always work head-uppermost on the trunk or branch, and are able to use their tail – which has evolved specially strong central feathers for the purpose – to provide additional perching support.

The diminutive, mouse-like Treecreeper also has strong central tail feathers which it uses like a shooting stick, and also works always head-up on the bark. It is not related to the woodpeckers but is a member of the Passeriformes (the vast complex of song and perching birds) and, like its relatives, has its toes arranged three forwards, one behind.

Another passerine sharing the tree-climbing habits of the woodpeck-ers is the handsome Nuthatch. Like those of the Treecreeper, its power-ful toes are arranged three and one, not two and two, but it lacks any tail modifications. In consequence, Nuthatches are to be seen head downwards on the trunk almost as often as head-up, as they place no reliance on their tail for additional support.

The amazing Dipper

Though operating in vastly different circumstances, another passerine, the Dipper, logically merits mention here. Dippers are birds year-round resident of fast-flowing, shallow, upland becks and streams that chatter

Dipper

over stony beds as they hurry down the hillsides. Anatomically Dippers resemble thrush-sized Wrens, with much the same perky posture. Always bobbing up and down, large white bib conspicuous, they characteristically perch, tail cocked, on boulders in mid-stream. Standing on its slippery rock, the bird's feet seem over-large and powerful, but with good reason as the Dipper has a fascinating feeding technique. As you watch, it slips off its boulder and submerges in the torrent with hardly a ripple. Once beneath the surface, it feeds on small fish and other aquatic animals like caddis fly larvae, water scorpions, shrimps and worms. Often it will walk along the bottom to catch these, hanging on with its powerful feet to resist the effects of its natural buoyancy and the current. In deeper water it may leave go of the bottom and swim, using its wings for propulsion, appearing silvery – if you are watching from a bridge spanning its stream – as it is encased in a thin sheath of air bubble.

Balancing acts: how birds perch

Last, and quite positively not least from the point of view of fascinating adaptation, we come to the great mass of the small passerines whose feet on superficial examination might merit the term 'general purpose' and which seem particularly to justify the colloquial name of 'perching birds' given to their order, the Passeriformes. Typified by a popular bird like the Robin, the passerines tend to have medium-length, relatively slender legs ending in four toes, three pointing forwards, one back.

Many of the passerines are largely arboreal – some of these, like the tits, renowned for their acrobatic capabilities among the twigs – while others are largely terrestrial, like the Meadow Pipit, spending much of its life (when not flying) running about actively on the ground in search of food. Yet others – the Great Tit and the Chaffinch come first to mind – seem to spend their time roughly equally down on the ground and up in the vegetation. Clearly there must be a number of subtle adaptive differences in leg and foot structure to cope with these varied life styles, though not perhaps so extreme as those in the Treecreeper, Nuthatch and Dipper.

Even many of the terrestrial passerines will, for safety's sake, fly up into bushes or trees when the time comes to roost overnight, and then they too join the others of their kind in exploiting the passerines' most fascinating leg and foot adaptation. When perching, to close its toes the Robin, for example, uses muscles in the upper parts of its leg to pull on tendons that run down behind the ankle (which looks like a reversed knee), down the tarsus and out to the toes. Its weight pushing down towards the perch tends to bend the leg at the ankle joint and exerts a bending action on these tendons, in turn clenching the toes and giving a firmer grip on the perch. So even if, while roosting, the Robin dozes off, it tends naturally to retain a firm grip on its perch.

However, the subtlety extends further than this, for the toe-operating tendons have an irregularly notched surface which runs over a series of ridges in the tendon sheath where it passes under the toe. The notches and ridges engage just like a ratchet fitted to a fisherman's reel, which, until positive action is taken to release it – by a deliberate movement on the bird's part – also tends to keep the toes clamped shut on the perch. Thus, awake or asleep, the Robin does not need to 'think' about using its perching ability, in much the same way as we do not need to think each time we draw in a breath.

Some quite unlikely birds also display perching prowess. Cormorants may often be seen perched on tree branches and have even been recorded as perching on power lines; and Herons in the heronry at the start of the breeding season, carrying branches with which to enlarge their nests, clamber about in the twigs, precariously but using the branch held in their beak almost as a tightrope walker uses his balancing pole!

Anatomy of a bird's wing

Of the limbs of birds, fascinating though their leg and foot adaptations are, it is tempting to consider that, as flight is such a vital feature of these creatures and their lives, the wings must be the more important and potentially the more fascinating. This may well be true: certainly the range of wing adaptations is no less diverse and interesting. Like the rest of a bird's skeleton, the wing bones need to be lightweight, but far more than elsewhere they must combine this lightness with strength.

When the wing is working, the strains fall directly on to the 'box

An eagle's wing skeleton and flight muscles

girder' structure of the thorax. The complex of bones forming the pectoral (shoulder) girdle is fixed firmly at only one point on each side to the thoracic box, and that is where the lower end of each coracoid bone is attached to the front end of the breast bone (sternum). The two shoulder blades lie alongside the backbone, and meet the coracoids at the socket where the wing is attached. They are braced together across the front by the collar bones, which are fused at their other ends to form the V-shaped 'wishbone'. Behind, the free ends of the shoulder blades are bound by stiff, strong ligaments on to the ribs and the backbone. This is the basis, the hinge as it were on which the wing proper operates.

The part that flaps is composed of three sections, each – though sometimes much modified – clearly also identifiable in the human arm. Attached to the shoulder blade by a strong ball-and-socket joint is the upper arm bone (humerus), a single long, strong, tubular bone. At its outer end – corresponding to the human elbow, but close to the body as often to be largely concealed by the body feathers – the humerus is jointed to the radius and ulna, two bones exactly paralleling those in the human fore-arm.

The third 'flapping' section is fundamentally a contracted assortment of wrist and hand bones; a small section of the wing called the 'bastard wing' or alula (important aerodynamically and paralleled by the slots on modern aircraft wings), composed of a few small feathers, is mounted on the vestigial thumb, and at low flight speeds can be seen to be held slightly forward of the main wing. The primary feathers are mounted on half a dozen small, flattened bones derived from what would have been the palm of the hand and the second digit.

The flight feathers

These primary feathers, usually between nine and eleven in number, are the outermost feathers in the wing. They are robustly constructed, firm yet flexible, and it is they that provide the forward propulsive force as the wing beats downwards. These are the feathers that look like fingers at the end of the broad wings of a Buzzard or, more familiar perhaps, on the wingtips of Rooks indulging in spring aerobatic displays over their rookery. Clearly they need to be reasonably rigid on the downbeat to push the air back and away to provide forward motion. On the upbeat, though, their flexibility comes into play as they twist and bend, allowing the air to pass easily between them and thus not immediately counteracting the thrust they have just produced. Each overlaps the next in a sort of 'Venetian blind' arrangement, with the narrower leading-edge vane overlying the broad rear vane of the next feather outwards in the wing.

Lift, the other essential element of flight, the force counteracting gravity and keeping the bird airborne, is produced in much the same way in birds as it is in man's aeroplanes. The inner 'half' of the wing is composed of the secondary feathers. The number of secondaries is very variable: small songbirds have six (plus three tertiaries), while in large soaring or gliding birds like Gannets, Storks and eagles, there may be dozens.

Irrespective of number, they have a common function: viewed end-on, the inner part of the wing has a convex upper surface and a concave lower one. This is called an aerofoil section, and when such a wing moves forward through the air (propelled by the primary feathers), because of its shape air moves faster over the upper surface than the lower. This creates a pressure difference between the upper and lower surfaces – the higher-speed air being at lower pressure – which in turn creates an upward force called lift.

The process is not quite so simple as it sounds, for moving an aerofoil through air may create turbulence, producing a drag force which tends to act in opposition to both lift and propulsive forces. Drag is overcome by careful positioning of the wing, and at low speeds by the use of the alula: all performed by birds instinctively and instantaneously, in marked contrast to the complex control mechanics necessary to achieve the desired results even in modern aircraft. In terms of flight capability there can still be no comparison between the flexible, almost infinitely variable wing geometry of a bird and that of the most sophisticated swing-wing jet fighter.

The muscles of flight

The massive muscles that power flight are located each side of the keel of the breast bone. Careful inspection as a chicken is being carved will reveal that there are two on each side, the outermost being much the larger. The problem with the chicken as an example is that both muscles are pale in colour, but should the fowl for lunch be a Capercaillie –

that huge forest-dwelling turkey-like member of the grouse family –
things are much clearer, as the smaller inner muscle is strikingly dark
in colour. The outer muscle (the pectoralis) is attached by ligaments
to the humerus and provides the pull for the all-important downbeat
of the wing. Less energy is needed to raise the wing ready for the next
beat – because the feathers twist and flex – so the raising muscle is considerably smaller. This smaller muscle (the supracoracoideus) lifts the
wing by an ingenious pulley system whereby its major tendon runs
behind the coracoid bone and then up and over the front of the shoulder
blade (which is the 'pulley') and back down on to the humerus.

Birds versus aircraft

If evidence were needed to support the argument that birds are 'better'
than aircraft, an examination of the various modifications of bird wings
during the course of evolution would certainly provide it. The wing
of a hummingbird, set in a socket allowing movement in almost any
direction, is perhaps the most efficient organ of flight in the animal kingdom, enabling the bird to perform aerial movements up, down, sideways, forwards and even backwards, as well as allowing it to perform
its well-known feat of hovering stationary in front of a flower from which
it will suck the nectar.

At the other end of the scale, in size as well as flight capability, is
the Ostrich, one of several flightless birds. The wing of an Ostrich is
still of use, though, as an organ of balance (important for a fast-running
bird), in display, and as a cooling fan during the hot African day.

Wing designs and their purpose

Throughout the bird families numerous other examples of wing designs
can be seen, each adapted to the life style of its possessor. Many can
be classed as 'general purpose' rather than specialist: the wings of a
large number of small songbirds like thrushes, finches and warblers fit
this category, as do those of most waders, ducks, gulls and terns.
Obviously there are differences – terns are longer and narrower in the
wing than gulls, for example, and tend to migrate over much greater
distances. Diving ducks have smaller wings and much faster wingbeats
than dabbling ducks – a feature useful in long-range identification. Of
the passerines, however, few stand out as highly modified for their daily
lives except the Swallow and the martins. With rather long, sickle-

shaped wings, they lead a high-speed, largely aerial life akin to that of the Swift (to which they are not related).

The Swift, with its extremely long, slender wings seems clearly built for speed. Its body is torpedo-shaped, rather wider at the front than the rear – a shape that modern engineers adapt for best streamlining – and its eyes are set into the body contours rather like a sports car's headlights. Much of the length of the wing is due to the primaries – the propulsive force – while the inboard section, carrying the secondaries, is relatively small. Thus lift is not great, and some speed is essential if the Swift is to remain airborne – hence, too, its difficulties in taking off from the ground. But this suits the life of the Swift, perhaps the most aerial of birds, eating, drinking, sleeping (or at least roosting) and even mating while on the wing.

Actually the Swift's wing is, in aerodynamic terms, better suited to energy-conserving flight at high altitude than to sustained high speeds, and this is borne out by records of the speeds of flying Swifts which, despite appearances to the contrary, fly at much the same sort of speed – around 40kph (25mph) – as many other birds both smaller and larger than themselves. Screaming parties of Swifts are familiar to town dwellers as they dash at apparent breakneck pace round the rooftops in summer; yet, fast as they are, they have a predator, the Hobby (one of the falcons) that can catch them in flight and thus must be even faster. In silhouette Swift and Hobby are remarkably alike except for the larger size of the falcon.

Hobby pursuing Swift

Fast falcons

The Hobby is one of several falcons, the Peregrine included, renowned for their speed in pursuit of prey, often over some considerable distance. At the other end of the scale, among the raptors, are the hawks, much rounder in the wing and often thought of as much slower. Though this statement may be broadly true, the differences are very much ones of degree and technique, for most hawks have very good powers of acceleration and can be pretty speedy over short distances. The differences in wing silhouette between the long-winged falcons and short-winged hawks are most meaningful when compared with their hunting strategies. The falcons are birds of wide-open spaces, flying down their quarry by sheer power, persistence and speed. The hawks, on the other hand, are scrub or woodland birds and must match the twists and turns of their prey as it dashes away for its life among the branches. Their rounded, heavily 'fingered' wings and long tail give them the power to apply a burst of high speed yet maintain great directional control.

An extreme example of wing manoeuvrability is found in the Hoopoe, an occasional visitor to Britain and Ireland but more common in southern parts of the Continent. Hoopoe wings are comparatively huge, rounded and heavily fingered, and their flight is slow and floppy enough to seem laboured. However, they are adroit in the extreme when it comes to flying among bushes, and to watch one avoiding the repeated stoops of an attacking falcon, side-stepping first one way, then another, with a burst of acceleration here or braking there – sometimes, it seems, almost going into reverse – is to marvel at yet another extremely effective avian adaptation.

The whirring wings of game birds

To escape quite different predators, most of the game birds too have rounded wings. Game birds are popular quarry to others besides mankind, not just because of their good taste but also because they have unusually large flight muscles which offer – as does the breast of a chicken – both succulent and easy eating. These flight muscles power rounded, deeply concave wings offering high 'lift', which the game birds use to leap swiftly into the air and away out of danger.

Partridge or Red Grouse, for example, will 'explode' from almost beneath your feet in the fields or on the moors and with whirring wings will accelerate away, quickly achieving maximum speed and then gliding onwards, almost like a missile, on down-curved wings, close over the ground. Such a technique gets them speedily out of reach of most

*Partridges
at take-off*

natural predators and makes them such a challenging target to a man armed with a shotgun that they are among the most popular of sporting birds. Where the Red Grouse is concerned, in shooting circles the opening day of the season, 12 August, the 'Glorious Twelfth', is *the* red-letter day – though doubtless the Grouse would not agree!

Because game birds are among the most terrestrial of avian creatures, it should come as little surprise that the young need special protection from predators. As would be expected, their development in terms of running about is precocious and they are admirably camouflaged. They leave the nest, running with the female, almost as soon as they are dry; and surprisingly, from the time they are half-grown (or less), should she take wing, the pint-sized youngsters with her do likewise, a unique feature in the world of birds.

Often to be seen in much the same habitats – fields, rough grassland and moorland – as Partridge and Red Grouse are Lapwings, unusual among waders for the roundness of their wings. With experience and practice, differences are detectable between the wings of male and female Lapwing as they fly overhead, those of the female being appreciably narrower. Called 'Lapwings' because of their floppy flight pattern, made the more emphatic by their striking black and white plumage, these birds draw attention to themselves in summer by their tumbling, diving, display flight and piercing 'pee-wit' calls.

At close quarters the rounded wings produce a marked whooshing noise especially their own, the male with his broader wings being noisier than his mate, as befits his role. In the breeding season, this wing noise comes into its own as a terror weapon to repel invaders in just the same way as screaming dive-bombers were used in wartime. Any marauding fox or crow – or even human – is instantly attacked as it enters the breeding territory. The swooping, screeching Lapwings, with these thumping wingbeats, are usually enough to put off – or at least distract – any predator and ensure the safety of the nest. The sight of a harmless pair of Partridges, straying accidentally into a Lapwing territory and then attempting to withdraw with dignity under such an onslaught, is one to be savoured.

Retaining the breadth of wing, but adding to it some considerable length, produces the flight silhouette so typical of the Buzzard and – though the bird itself is sadly much less often seen – the Golden Eagle. Such wings, with a long inboard section carrying numerous secondary feathers are ideally suited to the birds' way of life. These are the wings of a soaring bird, circling on high with hardly a wing flap, exploiting up-currents produced by thermals or by lines of hills or crags, scanning the ground far below for carrion or for the tell-tale movement of potential prey. Such a silhouette is typical, too, of many of the heron family and of the storks. Storks are long-distance migrants, travelling well south into Africa each winter from

Soaring eagle

European breeding areas. They migrate by soaring and gliding, waiting for the heat of the day to produce thermals, riding on which they spiral up to a great height then glide away south, gaining height again on any up-current they encounter. These thermals, or any other up-currents, are rare over the sea, and when it comes to crossing the Mediterranean, storks (and many of the birds of prey) select the 'short' sea crossings at Gibraltar and the Bosporus. Here they collect in spectacular flocks, often tens of thousands strong, waiting for the correct weather conditions to give them a quick ascent to a sufficient height over the land before planing away to the southern shore, there to gain height again in the thermals rising off the arid hillsides.

Accommodating the bird brain

So there are several requirements that a bird's skull must fulfil. First, it must be light; second, the loss of teeth and manipulating fore-limbs during the course of evolution must be compensated; and third, the brain – and the ears and eyes – must be accommodated and protected. The first need is met by the fact that few skull bones of birds are more than thin plates and struts; the second point is explored in Chapter 4; the third requirement is covered by the comparatively large ear and eye openings, restricting the brain case to the rear of the skull.

So large are the orbits holding the eyes that in many instances only a thin partition separates the two. As far as the brain is concerned, the areas dealing with sight and hearing are well developed; while that dealing with smell is much reduced, for this sense in birds is poorly developed and apparently little used. Understandably, the region dealing with movement co-ordination and balance is very well developed, but the area that deals with some so-called 'higher functions' – in humans including logic and aesthetic appreciation – is predictably small. None the less, some of these so called 'birdbrains' (so wrongly derogatory a term) are capable of navigating with pinpoint accuracy in most weathers to a wintering place in Africa and back, over forests, deserts, mountains and sea, to their nesting area in the succeeding summer.

Keeping a level head

Interestingly, the head is held very stably both in flight and when perched. Watch the garden Robin on a gently rocking twig: though its body moves with the twig swaying in the breeze, its head is normally held quite steady, with the neck stretching and contracting to allow this. Watch, too, a Mute Swan in flight. The powerful wingbeats produce quite a loud creaking sound, evidence of the input of effort; and, as they beat, the body pitches slightly up and down on a fore-and-aft axis. The head, however, is held level and steady – in much the same way as a gyroscope steadies an inertial navigational system – as it moves through the air, the movements of the body being absorbed, like gradually diminishing ripples in a rope, along the length of the neck.

Bird's-eye view

Most birds gain more information about their surroundings through their eyes than through all their other sense organs put together, and

in birds the design of the eye, shaped by evolution, has reached standards of perfection unmatched elsewhere. Birds' eyes are large: even in the Starling the eyes are, relatively speaking, about fifteen times bigger than in man.

The benefit of the larger eye size is that it provides both larger and sharper images, vital for birds' fast-moving life styles. This visual acuity makes itself apparent in the splendid sight of flocks of waders shimmering and turning in unison, like twists of smoke against an estuary sky. Closer to home, the aerobatic skills of huge flocks of Starlings never cease to amaze, as they circle in the evening light before going to roost on city buildings, turning with perfect synchrony and without any seemingly inevitable mid-air collisions.

Some birds, though, stand out above the others so far as powers of sight are concerned. The streamside Kingfisher, for example, plunging from its perch in the apparently simple task of catching minnows, must make adjustments as it dives for the difference in refractive index between air and water, and compensate for the apparent exaggerated shallowness if it is to secure its target. Not surprisingly, the birds of prey also fall into this category. Vultures soaring thousands of feet above the plains, scanning for carcases, must clearly have quite exceptional long-range vision, but one of the champions, even among champions, must be the Kestrel.

Middle-sized for a falcon, the Kestrel is familiar both because of its characteristic hovering posture when hunting and because it is almost as regular in occurrence in towns and cities as it is in the countryside or hunting over the 'new' habitat provided by motorway verges (see Chapter 4). The sheer hunting physique of the Kestrel is matched with advanced anatomical features, for the retina of the bird's eye, the light sensitive area receiving the images produced by the eye lens, is almost twice as thick as it is in most animals. This naturally allows more microscopic light-receptive cells to be packed in, and at the fovea (the most sensitive area of the retina) the Kestrel may have a visual acuity an astounding eight or ten times better than that in man.

Not only is superb visual acuity found among birds of prey, but also fantastic sensitivity at low light levels. The owls are leaders in this field

Kestrel and prey

and the Tawny Owl is typical of them. Plump and comfortable looking, the Tawny Owl is nocturnal, hunting on wings in which all the feathers have a velvety surface for silence. Beneath the large round head with its huge dark eyes, the skull seems to be built almost entirely to accommodate exceptional powers of hearing and of sight. Owls' eyes face straight forwards, like our own, for highly practical reasons. The fields of view of the two eyes overlap to produce 'binocular vision', enhancing the stereoscopic effect and allowing precise judgement of distance, immensely valuable to the hunter. The retinas of the eyes are richly endowed with rods – special cells for low light reception. In tests, owls can spot prey – dead, so that hearing does not come into it – 1.82m (6ft) away at a light intensity as little as one hundredth of what we would require.

Owl eye structure

So large are the eyes, and so strangely pear-shaped to cope with their low-light acuity, that they cannot move in their sockets as do the eyes of most birds and mammals. Instead the owl has an exceptionally flexible neck and can turn its head through 360 degrees, without strangling itself, to keep in sight of what is going on. For the Tawny Owl this is essential as most commonly it hunts from a perch. There it sits, well camouflaged, motionless apart from slow movements of the head. The moment prey is detected – a mouse or vole passing beneath the tree – the owl parachutes silently down on outstretched wings, talons spread for the kill.

Acute hearing

Many birds rely on their acute sense of hearing when it comes to locating prey: homely examples are the Blackbird and Song Thrush, every muscle tensed, head cocked to one side and a picture of alertness as they listen for the rustling, crunching microsound of a worm or a insect larva burrowing just below the surface of the lawn. On the beach the Ringed Plover listens in much the same way rather than following the repeated hopeful probing pattern of the Dunlin out on the mud, which relies on chance, the density of its prey and the sensitivity of its beak tip to obtain a meal.

Nowhere else in the animal kingdom are sounds so well exploited in communication as they are in birds, and this arguably includes comparison with man and his elaborately developed vocabulary. While our vocabulary is sophisticated in terms of dictionaries full of words in a multitude of languages, birds code their messages, as it were, in musical notation.

To us many bird songs are melodious in the extreme, and the many prose and poetic tributes to the quality of Nightingales' song testify to the aesthetic pleasure that it affords us. Few humans, though, would rhapsodize on the song of the Corn Bunting, sometimes likened to jangling a bunch of keys or shaking fragments of broken glass in a tin can! But slow down this apparently monotonous grating sound by four or even eight times – which is thought to represent best the acuity differences between birds' hearing and our own – and the elaborateness of the note structure thus revealed is quite stunning. It is still perhaps not music to our ears, but it does make it much easier for us to appreciate how birds can convey messages and instructions within the format of their songs and calls.

Sharp-eared owls

Once again it is to the owls that we must turn if we wish for the best examples of the acuity of avian hearing. Stripped of its feathers – including the facial disc so prominent in many owls, which functions like a cupped hand directing sounds into the ear – an owl's skull seems to consist mostly of largish beak, two huge eye sockets and two equally large ear openings, with little space remaining apparently in which the owl's legendary wisdom could be sited! Of immediate interest on the naked head (also visible if the feathers of the facial disc are pushed to one side) is the fact that the ear flaps – in themselves a unique refinement among birds – and orifices are not the same size and shape on each side of the head nor, come to that, are they in the same place.

The reasons are practical ones. As with early human range-finding devices relying on sound, a better appreciation of range is obtained if 'ear-trumpets' of different lengths are held to the two ears. (Much the same principle applies to the light-paths used by 'rangefinder' cameras.)

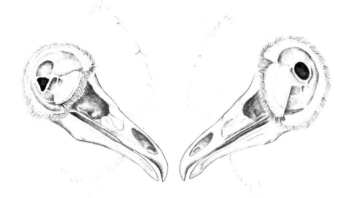

Owl ears seen from right and left

Owls' heads are relatively wide and in consequence sound reaches one ear a fraction of a second before the other, and this difference, coupled with the symmetry of the ears, also aids the precise location of sound. So good are these birds' ears that in experiments performed in total darkness in a light-tight room both Barn Owls and Long-eared Owls were able to pinpoint and strike mouse-sized prey, located by its tiny scuffling noises, several metres away.

Internal organs: the kidneys and gonads

Last in this chapter features the collection of internal organs, some of them associated in food processing with the skull and beak and all of them protected by the 'box-girder' structure of the thorax. Within the body cavity, located closed under the backbone, are paired kidneys. In their function, filtering waste products from the blood and excreting them in semi-liquid form, they are similar to the same organs in mammals, though what is excreted is largely uric acid rather than urea as in most mammals. In detailed structure the bird kidney shows more similarity to that of the reptiles than the mammals, but in stark contrast, as a reflection of the high-powered lives (in physiological terms) that birds lead, the kidneys are about twice the size of those in comparable mammals.

Most female animals have a pair of ovaries located close to each kidney, but strangely in birds usually only one, the left, is present full-size. Perhaps this is an adaptation to reduce weight for flight purposes, and it can be argued on the same grounds that this is the reason why the male reproductive organs (testes), though paired, shrivel to a minute size outside the breeding season. Copulation is achieved in most cases without the aid of a penis: the oviduct (in females) or sperm duct (in males) discharging into a large cloaca. When mating takes place, the male mounts the female with his tail depressed, while she raises her tail to one side. Their cloacas meet (often only very briefly) and the sperm is transferred. Brief though the contact may be, it is effective even in birds like the waterfowl – mating between ducks, for example, may take place with the female and most of the male submerged in water.

How birds digest their food

The alimentary tract, concerned with food processing, is normally long and coiled within the body cavity. Food is taken in by the beak, subjected to preliminary digestion with saliva and squeezed by muscle movements down the oesophagus (gullet) – a process clearly visible in the Heron or a swan. Some species like the Woodpigeon have a pouch-like crop for food storage linked to the oesophagus – in the case of the pigeon family this has thick glandular walls, and produces a protein-rich secretion ('pigeons' milk') used to feed the young.

The bird's oesophagus enters the thoracic box, passing behind the heart and expanding into a glandular stomach, where acid secretions hasten digestion. Behind the stomach lies the gizzard, hard and muscular and particularly well developed in seed-eating birds. In these birds, frequently the gizzard contains small sharp stones, specially eaten for the purpose of helping to grind up hard food in the absence of teeth. Some flesh eaters lack a gizzard entirely while others use it as a holding area, collecting fur and bones and other indigestible items prior to coughing them up as a pellet or casting.

Beyond the stomach and gizzard, the tract continues in a loop called the duodenum, where pancreas secretions change starches to sugars, and proteins and fats into simpler forms. Then follows the intestine proper, looping and coiling about the body cavity and particularly long in vegetarian birds. Here much of the food absorption into the blood takes place, the blood supply running first to the liver – where some food is stored away – to clean itself of toxic material before passing on to supply energy to the muscles. Often at the junction of the intestine with the rectum (a short wide tube leading to the cloaca, through which solid waste is voided) off-shoot blind pouches (caeca) may occur. These are particularly large in vegetarian birds and may help in the further breakdown of cellulose products, as well as assisting in the removal of water from the food.

In some birds whose diet may change from insects to fruit towards the end of the summer, or – like the Bullfinch's – from various relatively moist types of seed to those long-dried-out at the end of winter, the length of the gut, with its various absorptive sections, may change significantly with a change in diet and back again when the original food becomes once more available.

Some of the flowerpeckers, a group of birds well represented in Asia and Australasia and often called 'mistletoe-birds', feed on mistletoe berries and process their food with quite astonishing rapidity. They swallow the berries whole, and void the seeds as soon as a few minutes later. The extreme speed with which the berries pass though the digestive tract is only part due to their known powerful laxative effects! It is thought that a special stomach structure is more influential. The muscular stomach is set into action by a sphincter muscle from the oesophagus, so easily digested food (like the mistletoe berries) passes rapidly from the oesophagus direct to the intestine without entering the stomach, while other foods like insects and spiders that need grinding up and more thorough treatment with digestive juices, are digested in the stomach.

Circulation of the blood

Though the heart of birds, and indeed their blood too, is structured in a different way from that of the mammals – it has obvious affinities with the hearts of reptiles, from which quite clearly it has evolved – it is four-chambered, with a dual-circuit circulation which is apparently just as efficient. Blood, rich in oxygen from the lungs, enters the left side of the heart (auricle) and passes to the muscular left ventricle to be pumped round the body, delivering up its oxygen – necessary for muscle working – as it goes.

Spent, de-oxygenated blood is collected in a separate circulatory system from the muscles, liver and kidneys (where it has been 'cleaned up') and returned to the right auricle where it collects to be passed into the right ventricle, which pumps it back to the lungs to be recharged with oxygen. Though differing in finer details, the circulatory systems of mammals and birds, keeping oxygenated and de-oxygenated blood completely separate, allow these two groups to lead their high-speed, warm-blooded lives. Fish, amphibians and reptiles, with a two- or three-chambered heart able to pump only a mixture of fresh and 'used' blood, cannot maintain a high enough level of oxygen supply to live their lives at the same pace and thus remain cold-blooded and relatively sluggish.

Body temperature

Birds have a more rapid heartbeat than mammals and their temperature is usually appreciably higher, ranging from 37°C (98.6°F) in flightless birds like the Emu and Ostrich to 44°C (111.2°F) in smaller ones such as larks and finches. Like mammals, most birds for most of the time maintain this temperature consistently and independent of the surrounding air. There are exceptions, however: under some weather conditions, for example during an extremely cold night, the humming-birds that dwell high in the Andes find it difficult to maintain body temperature – in part because the laws of physics decree that small bodies with a relatively large surface area loose heat faster than larger bodies. On such cold nights the Andean hummingbirds become torpid: their breathing initially becomes rapid and they cease to fly, ultimately coming to rest perched head up, eyes closed and, it seems, barely breath-ing. Next morning, as the sun rises and begins to warm them, it may take upwards of half an hour for them to 'come to' from this torpor and recover their full flight agility.

The Poor Will, a New World nightjar, goes one stage further. Though many mammals hibernate in the true sense of the word, undergoing a winter torpor lasting for weeks or months, this physiological strategy is extremely rare in birds and indeed was only quite recently discovered. The Poor Will can hibernate for long periods in rock crevices to escape the rigours of winter, when food is scarce, and survive to the next spring. During hibernation the Poor Will's temperature drops to around to 5°C (41°F) and most bodily functions – pulse, respiration and so on – 'tick over' at about three per cent of their normal wide-awake rate.

Breathing and singing

For their highly paced lives, birds are in obvious need of an extremely efficient respiratory system to oxygenate the blood and to provide the total energy for living. Evolution has endowed them with a system unique in the animal kingdom in its structure, and one appreciably more than that of any competitor. The windpipe starts as a slit at the back of the tongue and runs down the neck, re-inforced by cartilaginous or bony rings, into the top of the thorax, by the wishbone, where it broadens into the voice box or syrinx. This is a chamber containing a band of bone and one or more taut membranes which act as vocal chords producing calls or song as air passes over them.

As would be expected, the whole syrinx is appreciably more complex, with more membranes, in noted songsters like the Nightingale, and much simpler in, say, the ducks with relatively simple quacking calls. Some birds – the Ostrich and several vultures amongst them – are to all intents and purposes voiceless, and in them the syrinx is hardly deve-loped at all. So this small structure is responsible for the voice of the Nightingale which, heard as a solo at dead of night, comes through the clear, warm, summer air as one of the most fabulous bird songs in the world. Certainly for most of us it is as near to perfection in British bird song as we are likely to get. Part of the thrill of listening lies in the variety of notes – from throaty chuckles to far-carrying whistles – and part in the tonal range, from rich cello-like phrases to the purest of treble trills.

Below the syrinx the system branches into two tubes, each of which runs to a lung, and beyond that into the unique series of air sacs – nine in total, four to each lung and one at the base of the throat linking the two sides of the system. These sacs are large, occupying a considerable proportion of the body space and in some cases penetrating into the central cavities of the larger bones. Compared with man, where the lungs occupy some five per cent of the body, in many birds the figure reaches twenty per cent. The lungs themselves are often relatively small, bright red and, in marked contrast to their mammalian counterparts, relatively inelastic. It is within the lungs that gaseous exchange takes place, but the extraordinarily high efficiency of the avian respiratory system depends more on the air sacs.

These sacs greatly increase the amount of air available to the bird, useful not just in breathing to obtain oxygen to fuel energy production, but also of great value if the bird is an expert at prolonged song, or indeed if it is a great diver. The precise way air is routed through the network of sacs is as yet improperly understood: what seems to happen is that they refill the lungs directly after breathing out, so that air is available for respiration continuously. On breathing in, fresh air enters the system and passes eventually to the lungs, resulting in a continuous flow system of oxygen-rich air passing through the lungs – not the 'on-off' method of breathing in and breathing out used by mammals.

This ability to extract oxygen continuously is exceedingly efficient and one that allows the birds to meet the high but vital energy demands of the flight muscles. Since birds cannot sweat – the imagination boggles at how bedraggled their feathers might appear if they could – a lot of the water exchange which helps to keep their temperature under control takes place over the inner surfaces of the lung's air sacs.

Though birds do have a diaphragm, a muscular wall dividing the thorax into two sections, this does not play a major role in breathing as does its counterpart in mammals, where movement of the diaphragm (like a pump plunger) at the base of a rigid rib cage controls the inhalation and exhaling of air. In birds it is the movements of the bulky flight muscles and expanding the air sacs and particularly the thoracic 'box-girder' that perform this task so effectively. Such a system automatically up-rates the supply when the bird takes wing and needs more oxygen, yet one more example of sophistication through evolution that has justly given rise to the title of birds as 'masters of the air'.

4 Food and Feeding

The power of flight is a characteristic feature of the great majority of birds and lies behind much of their success in that it has conferred the ability to reach new feeding areas – be they out in mid-Atlantic, up in the Arctic Circle, or simply far out on the topmost twigs of a tall tree – unavailable for one reason or another to most other animals. Flight has allowed great diversification in feeding, and indeed patterns of flight themselves are very diverse – but this has been achieved only at a cost. In taking on the power of flight, the birds have, so to speak, sacrificed their fore-limbs when it comes to other functions.

In many four-limbed animals – most of the grazing animals, other herbivores and, of course, seals and whales are the exceptions – to a greater or lesser extent the front pair of limbs play a vital role in food gathering. It may be that they are the carnivores' prime hunting weapon (the powerful front legs of the lion or the tiger used to wrestle prey to the ground and subdue it for the kill), or that they are used to extricate food from difficult surrounds, to remove inedible parts, or generally to manipulate food before eating – here the various monkeys and apes, and man himself, are the best examples. No matter what their food, it is only by adaptations of feeding techniques, of leg and foot design and of beak design that birds can cope with it, and because of the great diversity of bird diets these collective adaptations to securing food make a fascinating study.

Anatomy of a bird's head

The basic pattern of the avian skeleton – in this case it is the skull and the legs that are of prime interest – is remarkably uniform (see Chapter 3) compared with that of many other animal groups. An almost-spherical, thin-walled cranium is the general rule, with relatively large orbits holding the eyes – huge in nocturnal species. Beneath the main part of the skull is slung the lower jaw (mandible), composed, as in the birds' reptilian ancestors, of several bones. As in the case of the reptiles, the hinge of the lower jaw rests on two small, movable, often Y-shaped bones called the quadrates. Thus, instead of a simple hinge – like a door hinge – as found in the mammals, the birds have a double-jointed, wide-gaping articulation which helps, for example, the Puffin to hold several small fish in its beak and still to catch more.

In many birds, too, the upper mandible, also of several bones, is not firmly anchored at all points to the rest of the skull but is hinged on the forehead. This particular flexibility can best be seen in action when a member of the parrot family is tackling a tough seed.

Yet another general characteristic of the skull is that, unlike those of mammals, it joins the topmost of the neck vertebrae in a simple ball-and-socket joint, rather than in a double-knobbed and much less flexible knuckle. Even more flexibility is conferred by the neck, which may have many more component vertebrae than in mammals. In mammals, seven vertebrae is the typical rule, applying equally to the giraffe as to the bulldog, but among birds the number may reach twenty-five, as in the swans.

The two mandibles, upper and lower, carry the outwardly visible parts of the beak which are in effect horny sheaths. They, and the bone structure beneath, vary in size and shape depending on the food and feeding techniques of the bird concerned: obvious examples are the short, powerfully hooked beaks of the birds of prey; the long slender probing beaks of several waders; and the pyramidal (or wedge-shaped) beaks which typify seed eaters. In the case of the seed eaters, both the stoutness of the mandibles and the amount of skull musculature necessary to crush the food item are evidenced by the relative size of head and beak.

Exploiting the sea as a food source

Before discussing the range of adaptations of beaks, feet and feeding techniques, it may be useful to look briefly at one single habitat, the sea, and discover how varied are the feeding techniques of those birds exploiting it as a food source. Not only does a wide variety of ways of feeding lead to an efficient 'harvesting' of the food resources on offer, but it also helps to avoid undue and harmful competition between birds seeking food in the same environment. As a feeding environment 'the sea' can be crudely divided into four components: the air above, the water's surface, under water and the sea floor. Each of these can be more subtly subdivided, of course, and 'the sea' provides an example of an international habitat which embraces the maximum number of different feeding techniques.

The air above the sea is, not surprisingly, mostly a specialist environment where the 'secondary' feeding techniques employed by predators and pirates hold sway. Obviously, of the four feeding 'areas' of the sea the richest sources of food – fish and other marine life, particularly plankton – occur at or below the water's surface. Only the flying fish make an exception to this rule by occasionally bursting through the surface and gliding through the air for a distance before plunging back into the water.

Astonishingly, one of the largest of tropical sea-bird families, the frigate birds, are thought to have evolved with flying fish as a basic diet, though they exploit their great flying skills to consume many other items of prey including the in-flight snatching of unguarded nestlings from other sea-bird nests. Fast, powerful flight on long, sharply angled wings is aided by a long, deeply forked tail that provides great aerial agility, and the final element of dextrous hunting is achieved by a relatively long, flexible neck and a long, sharply hooked beak with which prey is siezed in mid-air.

The pirates, best exemplified by the skuas, though often also capable of self-sustenance by 'routine' plunge diving for fish, exploit the absence over the sea of true birds of prey and indeed seem to go a stage further than these predators. Larger pirates, like the Great Skua, will relentlessly pursue small sea birds – especially petrels, but up to the size of a Puffin – until either they catch up with them in mid-air or their quarry drops exhausted into the water, there to be caught and butchered: this is straight predation.

More common as a skua technique is aerial piracy, which skuas of all sizes are known to indulge in. Using their flying skills they select a home-going sea bird laden with food for its young and pursue it until it disgorges its load. So agile are the skuas that they can match each twist and turn of their victim and soon are provided with a meal; normally so fast are their reactions that the disgorged fish is caught before it reaches the sea! Sheer size is no protecton against skua attack. Even homeward-bound Gannets are harassed by Great Skuas, which may catch a Gannet's wingtip in their beak and attempt to overturn it in mid-air – this approach usually promptly produces the desired result in an otherwise stubbornly resisting victim.

A number of birds maintain an aerial life style but dip down to the surface of the sea for food items – usually small fish or planktonic animals. Most of these make only momentary contact with the surface – Little Gulls and Black Terns are examples – and have a characteristic dipping flight pattern, making only slow forward progress. Others do make prolonged contact: in the case of the Storm Petrel, the feet patter on the water surface and it is thought that this, and their moth-like wingbeats, help to maintain them at a more or less precise height above a very irregular, choppy water surface as they peck up planktonic food.

Even more remarkable are the skimmers, rather tern-like tropical birds with a lower mandible much longer than the upper one. These belong to the calm waters of sheltered inlets or lagoons and fly on a steady course low over the surface, with the longer mandible partly immersed and cutting a fine 'wake' across the unrippled surface. When a prey item is contacted, this is snapped up with a twist of the head before skimming is resumed.

While actually swimming on the surface, a number of birds employ a variety of techniques. Birds as diverse as the huge albatrosses and tiny phalaropes may simply grab suitable food items at or just below the surface, while the Giant Petrel of the Antarctic – and occasionally also the Fulmar of the northern hemisphere – is an avid and gluttonous scavenger, sometimes eating too much subsequently to take wing until part of the meal has been digested. The black-and-white-chequered Cape Pigeon of the southern oceans sucks in water and filters out food through its beak, while some prions, also in southern oceans, use a technique called 'hydroplaning'. With wings outstretched, breast on the water and beak open beneath the surface, the prion propels itself along like a sledge with powerful thrusts of its feet, scooping in food as it goes.

Sea birds that feed by plunge diving

Next come the plunge divers, where the bird starts off in the air, turning and plummetting down to vanish beneath the surface, but heading for a previously located target fish. The depth to which these plunges penetrate varies, as does the size of the target fish. Terns take the smallest fish and make the shallowest entry, while the huge Brown Pelican – however improbable it may seem – dives for larger fish which it scoops up in its huge beak pouch quite close to the surface.

The Gannet dives deeply, with its skull double-skinned and pneumatized and its eyes set in cushioned sockets, all to protect them from the impact of a plunge that may begin 30m (100ft) or more above the waves and take the bird several metres below the surface. There can be few more spectacular sights than a flock of Gannets diving one after another into a school of fish, taking flight immediately on returning to the surface and climbing to achieve enough height for another plunge. Amazingly, it seems that they rarely impale one another in the continuing excitement of the chase. At the end of such an orgy of fishing, many of the more successful Gannets – like the Giant Petrel – are so loaded with fish that take-off runs, pattering across the waves, become too exhausting and are abandoned while the speedy digestive juices start to reduce the load.

A further development of plunge diving is 'pursuit plunging', a technique used by several shearwaters including the Manx. A dive, often from no great altitude, is followed by underwater pursuit of the quarry, during which the pursuer is propelled by either wings or feet. A wide range of sea birds chase their prey by 'pursuit *diving*', often venturing to considerable depths and occasionally to 100m (330ft) or more. Among these are the northern-hemisphere auks, such as the Puffin, Guillemot and Razorbill, which use their wings for propulsion in much the same way as do their southern-hemisphere ecological counterparts, the penguins. Cormorants and Shags also dive from a swimming position on the surface, but tend to keep their wings pressed close to their sides, relying on their huge webbed feet for swimming power during the chase – all four toes are joined by the webs. Closer inshore and, like the others, submerging usually with hardly a ripple, are the bottom-feeding sea ducks such as the Common Scoter and the Eider, seeking shellfish in the seaweedy shallows and primarily also foot-propelled.

Apart from the ducks, all these sea birds are seeking plankton or fish of various sizes. By their hunting techniques, by the depths to which they dive, and finally by the size or type of prey they choose, they exploit in full the richness of the seas and yet avoid undue competition for the same sector of the resources. An excellent example of birds selecting differently within the same locality can be watched at any good mixed sea-bird breeding colony. The Kittiwakes will return to their nests largely with small planktonic items, while the closely related auks all take fish but of different sizes. Razorbills normally bring home a catch of many small fish, Puffins—several middle- to large-sized ones—and Guillemots—a single large fish—to feed their young. Gannets and Cormorants both take large fish, but the Gannet fishes further offshore and in deeper waters on mid-water fish, the Cormorant inshore, taking a considerable amount of sea-floor-dwelling flatfish.

Beak and foot adaptations: the diurnal birds of prey

When it comes to a review – which must be a selective one as the available examples are legion – of the structural adaptations of beaks and feet, and the accompanying behavioural adaptations associated with hunting and feeding techniques, to start with the flesh eaters, so often at the top of 'feeding pyramids' or the front end of 'food chains', seems as sensible as any other approach. Often called the kings of birds, the eagles – and, indeed, most other birds of prey – may in fact not live up as well as we would like to the powerful, noble hunting image that we have given them. Though all do hunt and occasionally take prey which is large compared to their own size, in many cases much of what they eat is either small and apparently insignificant (though nutritious) like beetles and worms, or carrion. Far from being degrading, scavenging on carrion, be it the carcase of a roadside casualty or the remains of a lion's kill, is an effective, energy-saving way of getting a meal with little risk to life and limb. The pursuit, at hectic pace, of quarry-twisting and turning over difficult terrain in its efforts to escape capture is a much more dangerous method.

But small or large prey items, carrion or not, the 'basic equipment' that the raptor needs remains much the same. Because of its powerfully hooked and ferocious appearance, it is tempting to assume that the beak is the major part of the weaponry. In fact, this is not normally the case, though on occasion the ultimate *coup de grâce* may be given by a bite at the base of the victim's skull.

A bird of prey's main aids are its talons: it is the legs, with four powerful toes, normally held in the shape of a cross to give maximum spread at impact and each armed with a long, curved and very sharply-pointed claw, that do the damage. At impact the claws close and frequently in the process penetrate a vital organ and incapacitate or kill the prey. The beak is normally reserved for feeding use, its hooked shape and strong construction allowing the tearing of flesh from the prey.

Birds, of course, have no teeth, and thus no ability to chew; so often, in the case of adult raptors, chunks of flesh and bone are bolted down in an ungainly manner. When it comes to feeding newly hatched young, however, even Golden Eagles – huge as they are – offer an extremely good example of just how delicately a massive beak can operate. Morsels of flesh smaller than a matchstick are torn from the carcase and offered with great gentleness to the weak and tiny nestling, at this stage itself hardly as long as its parent's beak.

The birds of prey rely on striking their quarry to achieve a kill. This strike may be in the air (as with falcons and hawks) or on the ground (as with eagles, harriers and buzzards), but in either case it is imperative that the kill is made without interfering with the predator's power of flight. One perhaps unexpected consequence of this is that almost all raptors have disproportionately long legs. Part of this length is clearly visible in the tarsus, the long, often yellow-coloured bone (in fact, two bones) running up from the toes to the joint which, though appearing in the mammalian knee position, is actually the bird's ankle. Less conspicuous, though equally elongated, is the feather-covered shin normally held largely concealed in the body feathers. It is only when a bird like the Sparrowhawk is seen to strike at and catch a small bird

in aerial pursuit that the length of leg can be seen, and a proper appreciation be possible of its function in keeping the struggling victim well
out of the way of the predator's wings which must continue to provide
effective flight.

Raptors like the harriers, gliding low over the reedbeds before plunging down on to some unsuspecting water bird or water vole, gain clear
benefit from long legs in not wetting, and perhaps thus waterlogging,
their plumage while feeding. Others, though, specialize in catching fish.
Worldwide in distribution, the Osprey is one of the best-known, plunging often with an enormous splash into a river or lake and emerging
shaking the water from its feathers to labour into the air with a large
fish, grasped head forwards torpedo-like, in its talons. Fish are particularly slippery prey, and the undersides of the toes of the Osprey – and
other fish eaters – are strikingly rough and knobbly, like coarse emery
paper, to give the best possible grip.

How the Kestrel feeds

Probably the most familiar bird of prey is the Kestrel, one of the falcons
and a bird that has adapted well in exploiting the new environments
made available by man both in towns and, particularly, along motorway verges. Falcons typically hunt using sheer speed: the Kestrel sometimes does, but more often relies on its specialist ability to hover, while
scanning the ground below for likely prey. While hovering, it beats its
wings and moves its tail to maintain station, but a close inspection
through binoculars will show that, even in a strong wind, its head
remains rock-steady. Kestrels have supremely good eyesight (see Chapter 3), evidenced by their ability to spot prey as small as beetles – let
alone voles – from heights sometimes in excess of 30m (100ft). Clearly
keeping the head, with its large eyes, steady must aid this operation
greatly.

Even the 'typical' falcons vary considerably in their hunting strategies. Fastest of all in level flight is probably the Hobby. With long,
powerful, sickle-shaped wings, it looks rather like a giant Swift, and
is even capable of outflying and catching Swifts in the air. Hobbies,
and the Red-footed Falcons of eastern Europe, also feed on large insects
like dragonflies, again caught in mid-air, but they show an unusual feeding habit of holding their catch in one foot and eating it while still in
flight, like a child would an ice-cream cornet – a further demonstration
of the adaptive use of long legs.

Up on the moors and in the mountains it is the small Merlin and
the much larger Peregrine that hold sway. For their size both are

robustly built but very fast. The Peregrine, for centuries certainly the favourite bird of falconers, who fly birds at quarry from a gloved fist, has the more spectacular technique. On a hunting expedition (captive or wild) the Peregrine will classically climb to a considerable height until almost lost to sight. High above it will wait, like a human fighter-plane pilot, circling and soaring gently on the up-currents, until a suitable quarry bird flies beneath. Its prey ranges in size from Ring Ousel to Golden Plover, Grouse and even the occasional goose. Then begins the famous stoop: initially the Peregrine will use its wings in a steep downward dive until maximum speed is reached – a speed extremely difficult to measure with accuracy, but probaby in excess of 160kph (100mph) though unlikely to reach the 320kph (200mph) sometimes claimed. At full speed it closes its wings almost tight against the body and plummets, full-tilt, talons outstretched, into its victim with a thud often audible a great distance away. Should it miss an adroitly dodging quarry, it needs must climb again to gain sufficient height for another power-diving stoop.

Maintaining the comparison with man's warplanes, the smaller Merlin follows an equally well-tried routine. These birds patrol their territory at moderate flight speeds and at low level over the heather. Should they flush potential prey – almost inevitably small birds like Meadow Pipits – or come across such a bird in flight, they accelerate to attack from behind, climbing slightly and attempting to achieve a kill after a brief, high-speed chase.

Brief, high-speed chases are also the tactic of the hawks, but the terrain in which they are carried out is vastly different. Sparrowhawks tend to wait, perched, or to cruise slowly through often quite dense woodland until suitable prey comes within range. The falcons are characterized by long, pointed wings that provide sheer speed, often over a distance, whereas the hawks have much broader, rounded wings with conspicuously 'fingered' tips where the flight feathers are splayed apart. This format allows quick acceleration for a start, but more particularly confers an agility and manoeuvrability on the Sparrowhawk that allows it to match the twists and turns of its quarry – often a tit, finch or thrush – as it darts in and around the trees and bushes.

The owls: superb night hunters

Only slightly different from the diurnal (daytime-hunting) birds of prey are the owls. The 'tools of the trade' are much the same – a hooked beak for tearing up the flesh before eating it, and long legs ending in powerful, widely spread, four-square talons for the actual capture and kill. Where Kestrels' eyes reach their peak of acuity for daytime vision, the owl family have eyes specially evolved and adapted to give superb poor-light vision. Good though their eyes are in the gloom, however, owls cannot 'see in the dark' if the dark is genuine, but they can still in many cases continue to locate their prey with considerable accuracy by means of remarkably acute hearing. This is described in more detail in Chapter 3.

Most owls hunt on silent wings – a necessity if the noise of feathers moving across one another, or through the air, is not to drown the more-distant scufflings of the prey. This silencing is achieved by means of a filamentous feather surface, velvety to both the eye and to the touch. In addition the leading edge of the foremost flight feather has barbs of unequal length, arranged so that the edge cutting into the air more resembles a comb than a knife. These comb-like projections create air currents that muffle the whooshing sound of the wing beating through the air. Though the longer-winged owls – Barn and Long-eared, for example – hunt most often on the wing, others, like the ubiquitous Tawny (or Brown) Owl commonly hunt from a perch commanding a good view and a wide listening area.

Owls eyes are top-shaped, not spherical, and so highly adapted and large that they cannot move in their sockets. In consequence a perched Tawny Owl must move its head from side to side, through almost 180° each way, to scan for prey. This movement of the head like a radar scanner also helps the bird locate sound. Here again the velvety feather surfaces play an important role in ensuring that the noises of movement do not obliterate more vital sounds. The similarity to a radar scanner can be carried further: the 'facial discs' of rather stiff, bristle-like feathers to be seen around an owl's eyes, besides giving it its typically owl-like face serve more practically to reflect (as does a sound recordist's parabolic reflector) the smallest of noises into the huge ear openings located just behind them. Those owls which hunt from a perch tend to wait for prey to pass beneath – often, though not always, actually on the ground – before parachuting down, talons outstretched, to make a kill. They tend to have short, rounded wings ideal for such a flight.

One feature, actually widespread among birds that consume whole prey with a considerable indigestible component (bones, fur, feathers, and hard insect parts like the wing cases or elytra of beetles), is best known

Long-eared Owl

from the owls. This is the process of regurgitating the indigestible remains as a casting, usually called a pellet. Small insect-eating birds produce pellets about the size of a pea, but in most owls they are about 5×3cm ($2 \times 1\frac{1}{4}$ins), some larger, some smaller. Characteristically owl pellets are grey-brown and rather furry, and they can be dissected to reveal various bones from the prey. Some of these – for example, the skulls and jaws of small rodents – can be readily identified, so an analysis of pellet content can offer some guidance as to the make-up of an owl's diet in a particular area or habitat, or at a particular time of year. Of course, not all prey taken leaves such visible and identifiable remains – earthworms, for example, do not.

The fish-eating herons

Not all flesh eaters have hooked beaks, nor do they all rely on talons for the kill. The heron family specialize in eating fish and other aquatic or waterside animals ranging from ducklings and water voles, through frogs and newts, down to large leeches. The herons are long-legged, long-necked water birds, almost always relying on a swift, stabbing strike with a large, dagger-like beak that may transfix or simply grab the prey. Considered worldwide, the members of this family are numerous and varied, especially in size, and provide in many cases further examples of how a feeding habitat – in this instance wetland – is effectively exploited without undue competition.

In Africa dwells the biggest heron of them all, the Goliath, almost man-high, which wades deep in lakes – far out of the depth of its relatives and stabs fish far too large for the others to tackle: 40 or 50cm (15 or 20ins) long and wide-bodied. Remaining in Africa, the Grey Heron (just 'Heron' to Europeans) wades in similar waters but closer to the shore. Closer still is to be seen the medium-sized, extremely slim Purple Heron, which has a fascinating hunting technique. It wades slowly and sedately, so as not to disturb its prey, but in addition keeps its neck outstretched and body held slim and upright, pointing always at the sun, to minimize any shadow that it casts and to keep that shadow around its feet, again to avoid giving advance warning of its presence to unsuspecting prey. Even its dagger-like beak is held 'nose-in-air', but this seemingly improbable posture does not, as might be expected, severely restrict its vision of the water, for heron's eyes bulge out from shallow sockets and can swivel to look straight down when the beak is pointing almost straight up.

In striking contrast is the Black Heron, a rather smaller bird restricting its feeding to weedy shallows where the water is only a few centimetres deep. This bird's feeding technique is to run a few paces then pause, meanwhile extending the wings and arching them forwards to produce a fairly precise replica of a parasol. The heron remains crouched in this umbrella-like posture for up to a minute, often less, and may take a stab at a small fish beneath its canopy. It is debatable whether what the Black Heron is doing is creating a patch of cool shadow into which potential prey might be lured to shelter from the hot African sun, or – as a human might when confronted with bright light reflecting off the water – using its wings to create a sunshield, so that it can see prey better underneath it. So brief is each umbrella pose before the Black Heron darts off to its next stance that the second theory perhaps seems more probable.

Three other small herons occur along the shores of African lakes (and other lakes elsewhere, even in southern Europe). They are very similar in size and could on first inspection seem likely to be competitors for food. The Squacco Heron frequents waterside vegetation, walking slowly or sitting, neck hunched down between shoulders, until an unwary frog strays too close, when the neck is unleashed to full length and the unfortunate prey is siezed and swallowed whole, alive and kicking.

Though similar in size, and in structure in most other respects, the Night Heron has much larger eyes than its relative and these are the key to its feeding style. During the day, it roosts in trees or reedbeds – where often the Squacco Herons will roost at night – and as dusk falls it will fly out to the lakesides, passing the Squaccos on their way to roost. Large eyes and good poor-light vision allow the Night Heron to hunt on when others must depart – again a mechanism avoiding overlap of feeding habitat and food-source competition.

Cattle Egret and wildebeest

Last of the three is the Cattle Egret. Again, almost identical in size and shape to the Squacco Heron, it can and sometimes does behave in a routinely heron-like manner by hunting fish and frogs along the lake margins. Far more often, though, it is to be seen on arid plains and fields a long way from the nearest water, feeding on large insects like grasshoppers. Ancestrally Cattle Egrets are associated with the antelope herds of the African plains – as they still are – as well as with elephant and buffalo, often riding on the larger animals' backs and removing the ticks from their hide. The main lure, however, is the grasshoppers disturbed by the beasts' hooves which provide a readily available food source, and it is easy to see how the bird got its colloquial name when it extended its riding habit to domestic cattle. But the adaptability of the Cattle Egret did not stop there: the advent of tractor ploughing meant that a new food source – worms and the like – became available, and this Cattle Egrets were quick to exploit, following the plough as gulls do elsewhere.

Exploitation and teamwork

Exploitation has not been one-way, though. In Japan another fish-eating bird, one of the larger Cormorants, has for centuries been taken as a nestling from its breeding colonies – by a special 'guild' of fishermen – and raised in captivity. When the Cormorant is mature, the fisherman sets out with several perched on the gunwale of his boat, each with a collar round its neck attached to a long lead. The collar is tight enough to prevent the Cormorant swallowing the larger fish it catches, and on its return to the boat it is relieved of its capture by its fisherman master and sent off to fish again, after some time being rewarded with a small tit-bit. Its appetite is not allowed to be satisfied with a good meal until its master has secured the catch he wants.

Exploitation is but a step distant from team work. Team work in birds when a group of the same species operates synchronously and with a common goal, is rather difficult to define, especially if human parallels are sought with overtones of 'unselfish' behaviour. It is probably simplest to assume that some birds have discovered that, by operating in groups and in a more or less co-ordinated manner, they each satisfy their goal of keeping well fed!

Water birds provide at least two examples of this sort of team approach. Spoonbills have, as their name suggests, long beaks with a spatulate ending, rich in sensory receptors. They feed in shallow, usually muddy water and tend to rely on these sensors to locate, and remain in contact with, prey, rather than using their eyes. Flocks of African

Spoonbills will often gather to 'round up' fish, running through the water and herding a school of small fish into a nearby bay. They keep in contact with the fish by immersing their beaks, occasionally grabbing and swallowing one, but this can have comical results if the school eventually turns and flees between the legs of the advancing birds, which then find that their heads must accordingly turn between their legs which are still running in the opposite direction.

White and Dalmatian Pelicans, too, often hunt as teams, usually six to a dozen or so strong. Initially, out on the lake, they swim in a stately open-mouthed 'U' formation. There is probably no formal 'leader' of the team giving the signals but, possibly activated by the movements of the hungriest member of the party, they smoothly form into a circle, simultaneously plunging their huge pouched beaks deep below the surface, raising their wings to provide a counterpoise to prevent themselves overbalancing on the water. This process of herding the fish within the arms of an outstretched net, and then closing off the entrance and encircling the fish, has also been used by man since biblical times, and has more recently been called seine netting. Again simultaneously, but without obvious signal, all heads re-emerge from the water, and those with fish in their pouches swallow them. The birds then set off to repeat the process.

From some habitats, and particularly some substrates, mankind would find it extremely difficult to extract the prey items that birds feed on. We can use a variety of hooks, nets and fishing techniques to catch most of the spectrum of fish exploited by fish-eating birds, and indeed are now doing so. Low-grade meal produced from this fish forms a protein-rich feed for our farm animals. Unfortunately, as a result fish stocks, and thus nearby sea-bird colonies, are locally under severe threat. Yet there is still no way in which our fishing expertise can match that of the wide range of waders which visit our coasts and estuaries, securing their prey – normally worms, shrimps or shellfish – from the most glutinous mud.

Once again, the picture is a clear one which can readily be observed by any birdwatcher prepared to journey to the nearest estuary: it is one of anatomical and behavioural differences, some gross, some subtle, shaped by evolution to maximize the harvest to be taken from the habitat while spreading the load right across that habitat – and thus minimizing competition. We must remember, too, that coastal feeders are governed by tide and not by daylight, so the waders must be able to feed in the near-dark. As they locate their prey usually below the surface of the mud and by touch, using nerves in the sensitive tips of their beaks, this is less problematic than might at first be imagined.

Waders small and great

At the top of the sandy shore, often some distance from the high-water mark and among the various maritime plants able to survive in the exposed and salty splash zone, are to be found birds like the Ringed Plover. Small in size for a wader, and with the characteristic plover short beak, this bird darts about picking up all manner of small invertebrates from marine isopod crustaceans resembling woodlice to shrimps and terrestrial – rather than marine – beetles.

Only rarely will the Ringed Plover probe, but its much larger relative, the Grey Plover – which has one of the most soulful cries of any bird – feeds well out on the mud or sand flats. Although still *relatively* short, the beak of the Grey Plover is perfectly adequate for shallow probing for surface-layer shellfish. Recently some Grey Plovers have been shown to establish winter feeding territories, and to defend these against others of their kind: an unusual feature, but one likely to enhance the survival chances of the individual concerned, especially if it returns to the same 'territory', which it knows well, in subsequent years.

Another feeding technique employed by some members of the plover family, is called 'foot pattering'. The feeding plover pauses, alert, and, standing on one leg, vibrates the other leg and foot up and down at high speed. It is thought that this in some way encourages potential prey to come to the surface, the easier to be caught. A similar approach by Lapwings – and some thrushes – on grassland has been suggested as mimicking the fall of raindrops, which brings earthworms to the surface.

At the edge of the sea on a sandy shore – literally on the edge of the waves, scampering down the beach as the wave recedes and rushing back again in front of the next surge – is to be found the Sanderling. Characteristically white below and silver-grey above, this bird also has a short black beak and twinkling black legs which move so fast that they seem a blur. Sanderlings get their living because of their speed: food for them are the various small marine animals exposed by the breaking wave – but only briefly exposed before either reburying themselves or before fresh sand is swept over them by the sea.

In muddier estuaries, the medium-beak-length waders are best represented by the Redshank – also one of the noisiest and most alert of birds and not for nothing called the 'sentinel of the marshes'. Redshanks use their straight, quite fine beaks for probing to 3 or 4cm ($1\frac{1}{4}$–$1\frac{1}{2}$ins) for small annelid worms and molluscs, but are quite capable too of feeding by picking various forms of animal life, including trapped insects, off the surface of pools. The slightly larger Spotted Redshank specializes rather more in wading up to its belly to feed, both off the surface and by plunging its head beneath the water.

Even the two Godwits regularly seen in Europe – Black-tailed and Bar-tailed – though enjoying beak lengths sometimes in excess of 12cm (4¾ins), commonly plunge their beaks so deeply into the mud that their faces, and sometimes even their eyes, are immersed. Longest of all probing beaks on the European shore, however, and shaped like a letter 'J' is that of the Curlew, which may exceed 15cm (6ins). During the summer months the Curlew finds its long beak equally as effective as when the ground is softer, for then it seeks worms on the bogs or wet moorland where it breeds. Other waders also spend much of their time on swampy land, often well away from the shore. One such is the Snipe, for its size one of the longest-beaked of all birds, its overall length being just over 25cm (10ins) of which the beak accounts for up to 7cm (2¾ins) or twenty-five per cent!

Perhaps the most distinctive anatomical feature of the Snipe, apart from its characteristic zig-zag flight path and inordinately long beak, is not readily to be seen except on a skeleton. Most long-beaked birds, probing deeply into soft mud for worms and other invertebrate animals, have the problem of avoiding eating large quantities of mud as well as their prey. In the Snipe, Woodcock and some others this problem is solved by a combination of slender, flexible nasal bones – supporting the greater part of the beak – and the small double-jointed quadrate bone in the angle of the jaw. By rocking the quadrate forward, the Snipe 'pushes' the tip of its beak forward – but only so far as it is also attached, via the nasal bones, to the forehead. As a result of this pushing, and the tension of the nasal bone, the tip (and only the tip) of the beak lifts back, enabling the Snipe to seize the prey it has located – using the many sensory nerves around the rather bulbous, fleshy tip to its beak – without taking in an inordinate amount of mud.

The adaptable Oystercatcher

Bridging the gap between rocky and sandy or muddy shores – by the simple expedient of exploiting both! – is the Oystercatcher. Colloquially called 'sea-pie' because of its striking black-and-white plumage, this bird shows a series of surprisingly specialist life styles. In the breeding season the wet valley-floor pastures of northern Europe are dotted with pairs of Oystercatchers, surviving well on a diet of worms extracted from the soil and, recent research would indicate, also breeding more successfully than their coastal cousins because inland they escape the predatory attentions of nearby Herring and Greater Black-backed Gull colonies.

Such primarily worm-feeding Oystercatchers can also flourish on estuary mudflats, as can those which tend to 'specialize' in feeding on cockles on the sandflat of sheltered bays like the Burry Inlet in South Wales. Here from time to time argument rages as to whether the Oystercatchers are 'robbing' the fishermen who dig on the sandflats for cockles for the local seafood industry. Usually the argument is triggered when particularly large numbers of Oystercatchers are to be seen and demands are then made for some form of cull. Normally, however, it seems that high Oystercatcher numbers are an indicator of an abundance of cockles, sufficient for both man *and* the birds to share.

Viewed from the side, the Oystercatcher has a medium-long, stout, straight beak. Viewed head-on, the beak tapers quickly towards the tip, which is slim and scissor-like, ideal for slipping between the shells of a bivalve mollusc like the cockle and snipping the adductor muscle that clamps the two valves together. Once this muscle is cut, the valves are easily opened and the bird quickly cuts out and eats the shellfish within.

Worm-eating Oystercatchers have rather more robust, less scissor-like beaks; and the last category, the limpet-eating Oystercatchers, naturally favour the weed-covered rocky shores where limpets abound and use the same techniques as any schoolboy when catching their prey. A quiet approach is followed by a swift, heavy tap from the beak, dislodging the limpet before its powerful emergency suction can secure it clamped to the rock. Once off, again it takes only moments for the bird to snip the limpet from its shell and consume it. Of just as much interest as this range of feeding techniques is the tendency of Oystercatcher parents to train their young in the same strategies as they themselves practise.

Other shoreline birds

Also to be found on the rocks of the shoreline, though often not without difficulty as their camouflage is so effective, are the dowdy Purple Sandpiper – often right among the surf and breaking waves – and the rather more colourful Turnstone, usually discovered on banks of rotting seaweed. Both of these are dumpy, short-beaked birds, the Turnstone with its beak flattened somewhat from top to bottom like a shovel and sometimes used, as befits its name, to overturn pebbles to catch small

Turnstones

animals beneath. More often Turnstones work their way through heaps of elderly seaweed, seeking the maggots of flies breeding in the rotting morass so unpleasant to human bathers. Their flat beak is just as effective on seaweed fronds as on stones. Besides their more normal small marine animal diet, Turnstones are among that wide group of birds that on occasion turn to any nearby carrion as a food source. There are numerous records of Turnstones feeding on the carcases of dead sea birds, and even once on a dead cat. Sheer versatility must account for the Canadian record of one feeding from a dead wolf, but the ultimate in necrophagous behaviour must be the record of a Turnstone in North Wales feeding from a long-drowned human corpse washed up on an Anglesey beach.

Specialization of a more predictable – and acceptable – nature also occurs among the waders. At the simplest end of the scale must be the Woodcock, structurally akin to the Snipe but most atypical for a wader in that it spends much, or perhaps all, of the year in damp deciduous woodland, clearly finding adequate food in the earthworm population. The Avocet, which sweeps its slender up-turned beak from side to side through shallow water or liquid mud shows both structural and behavioural departures from normal wader approaches, as does the Red-necked Phalarope.

In the breeding season phalaropes frequent shallow pools in northern Europe and on the Arctic tundra. They swim very actively and buoyantly, paddling frantically with toes lobed along their margins like miniature Coots. Among the plethora of waders exploiting the summer richness in insect food they have developed an aquatic speciality, perhaps because the marshy terrestrial habitat is used to the full by more robust or belligerent birds, ranging in size from Little and Temminck's Stints and Dunlin up to Godwits and Golden and Grey Plovers. Besides picking food off the water surface with a short, needle-fine beak while swimming, the Red-necked Phalarope's speciality is to twirl round

Avocets

and round on the spot, stirring up an eddy that lifts food items – otherwise out of reach on the floor of the pool – to the surface where they can be captured and eaten. It makes, in effect, a whirlpool in reverse.

The feeding techniques of wildfowl

Before moving away from the shorelines, mention should be made of that other large group of birds whose specialist habitats are water, wetlands and their surrounds – the wildfowl. All are characterized by a typically 'duck-shaped' beak and by feet webbed between the three forward-pointing toes. Interestingly, the short and sturdy legs are set well towards the tail in those that are almost entirely aquatic (for example, the sawbill ducks); nearer the tail than the breast in most ducks, which, like the 'typical' Mallard, regularly emerge from the water, not too clumsily either, to feed, rest or preen; and almost centrally – under the centre of gravity – in those species (especially the geese) which spend a great deal of their time grazing on dry land.

Starting with the species favouring drier habitats, these are largely a range of grey geese, all with a relatively long but very flexible neck and a tough, sharp-edged, wedge-shaped beak suitable for nibbling grass; or, if the beak is rather bulkier like that of the Greylag (ancestor to our farmyard geese), various roots and tubers, including the left-overs after potato harvesting. The Barnacle Goose, one of the so-called 'black' geese, is almost entirely confined to grazing the short sea-washed sward of the turf of coastal marshes (or 'merse'), but perhaps the main fascination of this bird lies more in its associations with human gastronomic folklore than with actual avian diets.

For many centuries the Barnacle Goose was linked with the 'goose barnacle', a rather strange but widespread marine crustacean. Bigger than related species that encrust seaside rocks, goose barnacles are set on fleshy stalks and have segmented shells within which a shrimp-like creature is housed, lying on its back and kicking food into its mouth with tiny, feathery feet when the shells are open. Ancient herbalists and others, including Giraldus Cambrensis writing in 1185, vouchsafe to have seen – usually in Scotland or Ireland – with their own eyes tiny or part-formed geese emerging from these shells. These were then supposed to increase in size and grow feathers to mature into Barnacle Geese. As they were averred to be more akin to fish than flesh, the powerful religious scruples of the time about meat-eating during periods of fasting, like Lent, could safely be put to one side in the case of the Barnacle Goose. Perhaps it is no coincidence that Giraldus Cambrensis travelled to Ireland and discovered these convenient zoological eccentricities 'exploited by bishops and religious men' to tide them over the otherwise very dull meatless periods in company with Prince John, noted for his gluttony.

The related Brent Goose, smaller and darker, had until recently the reputation of being highly specialist in its diet in winter, feeding very largely on a strange marine grass called *Zostera*. In the last decade a series of good Arctic breeding seasons have seen a huge increase in Brent Goose numbers to levels far in excess of those supportable by the *Zostera* and a few favoured marine algae in European estuaries. With little hesitation the Brent turned to winter wheat growing in nearby fields, to the concern of farmers and conservationists alike as on occasion crops were damaged by the heavy grazing. Whether this was a genuinely new feeding technique, or whether recent schemes to drain coastal marshes, previously rough grazing – and of no interest to the Brent – and convert them to more profitable arable cropping presented the geese with an acceptable diet that had previously been 'out of reach' inland, is difficult to discern. Certainly, though, such events highlight the need for a detailed ecological 'think-through' of the full implications of such otherwise tempting marginal land improvement schemes, because deterring the birds, or preventing damage, is a notoriously difficult operation once they have discovered the new food source.

Though it is the geese that most regularly feed on dry land – the grey geese in particular – all the swans, Mute, Whooper and Bewick's, will regularly graze lush pastures and sometimes growing cereals. This

causes displeasure to farmers not, as might be expected, because of what they eat, but more because their considerable weight and large webbed feet compact muddy ground, interfering with the natural surface drainage and creating puddles of waterlogged soil which later dry out to a brick-hardness equally unsuitable for plant growth. Actually a small amount of grazing, controlled and spread over the whole crop, encourages the growth of more cereal shoots (tillers) and improves the crop: this is the reason why sheep were often turned out on to winter wheat in its early growth stages on the old mixed farms.

Dabbling and diving ducks

Some of the ducks, too, venture on foot away from the water's edge, particularly the Wigeon, which gets much of its food requirement from the lush grasses and tubers on the marshland. Most of the other 'surface feeding' – or, more attractively, 'dabbling' – ducks feed in the shallows or in waterside soft mud. Most are predominantly vegetarian and seek as their prime food the seeds of various aquatic plants, especially reeds and sedges. The feeding area is partitioned in part by food choice and structural adaptation – the huge, spoon-shaped beak of the Shoveler, filtering food items from the mud by squishing it out over the lamellae fringing the beak, is the best example – and in part by the size of the bird.

Feeding waterfowl: from left, Tufted Duck, Mute Swan, Pintail, Mallard, Teal, Wigeon

Thus the Teal, smallest of European ducks, is to be found in the shallowest water or often just sitting happily on the mud, passing it through its beak, while the larger Mallard will be rather further out, often up-ending to reach the bottom. Further out still, and again up-ending frequently, will be the beautifully plumaged, slim and elegant Pintail. The Pintail's long neck stands it in good stead by allowing it to feed in deeper water than the other dabbling ducks, but the ultimate 'up-ender' must be the Mute Swan, which can easily reach food seeds on the bottom, and aquatic plants, in water a metre or more in depth.

Operating in waters too deep for up-ending is the other major duck group, appropriately (in view of their feeding technique) colloquially known as 'diving ducks'. By far the best-known of these are the relatively small, dumpy Tufted Duck, perhaps more conspicuous because of the drake's pied plumage than his drooping crest; and the Pochard, where the drake is a sombre but attractive mixture of chestnut, grey and black. On many inland waters, especially larger ones, the two species commonly occur together, though elsewhere the Pochard is regularly found on saline waters, especially estuaries, the Tufted Duck rarely so. On fresh waters both species tend to be omnivorous, taking plant and animal matter as available, but the Pochard rarely dives below a metre or two, while the Tufted Duck not only normally dives rather deeper than this – regularly up to 3m (10ft), occasionally even deeper – and understandably tends to be under water for longer.

Far more specialist anatomically are the fish-eating ducks, the 'sawbills', so called because their long, slender, sharply hooked beaks are edged with backward-pointing serrations that help them to grasp their slippery prey. The two most numerous sawbills, the Goosander and the Red-breasted Merganser, though relatively large among the ducks, are very torpedo-shaped in the body for good underwater streamlining, and as a further adaptation to hunting fish beneath the surface have their feet set well back on the body to provide the most powerful propulsive force. Small groups of both species will patrol swimming on the surface but with their heads immersed looking for prey.

Yet another set of adaptations is shown by the sea ducks, marine species typified by the large, heavily built Eider. At first glance perhaps the most striking difference between the Eider and other ducks is its beak. While other ducks have a clearly demarcated horny beak set, as it were, on the front of the head, or face, the beak of the Eider seems to merge with the skull, and areas of feathering run well down towards its tip. The whole profile of the Eider head is wedge-shaped and very robust, and the areas of feather-covered flesh extending on to the beak are part of the powerful musculature that the Eider needs to crush its standard prey of molluscs, quite commonly bivalve mussels. These are obtained by diving in the shallow seas just off the coast. Feeding is especially vigorous towards low tide when such food is more easily obtained.

Terrestrial flesh eaters

Terrestrial flesh-eating birds at the upper end of the size scale – the birds of prey and the herons – have already been considered, but those selecting much smaller prey items should also be mentioned. It is convenient to call these species 'insectivorous', although most if not all of them will eat far more than just insects, taking a wide variety of other arthropods – spiders and the like – as well as the occasional mollusc, crustacean (such as freshwater shrimps) and, particularly, annelid worm. Insects and most other arthropods are much more active and abundant – and thus more easily caught – during the warmer months of the year, surviving the cold months of winter as eggs, as larvae (often in some form of pupa), or as adults, hidden well away in dark, sheltered crevices where the microclimate is less harsh and the risks of discovery by a predator are minimal.

Even soil invertebrates – insect larvae again, and worms – tend to migrate downwards in frosty weather below the surface of the soil which is in any case often frozen too hard for easy penetration by a bird's beak. It is only in extremely severe spells of winter weather that the salty water and mud of an estuary will freeze, so the waders and ducks dependant on invertebrate animals from the same groups – but inhabiting marine surroundings – do not normally have the same food-finding problems that confront terrestrial insectivorous birds every winter over much of Europe.

The insect eaters

Treecreeper

In many cases – the Great Tit offers an excellent example – birds which are primarily insectivorous during the warmer months avoid confrontation with this food problem by turning far more to vegetable foods like fruit, seeds and nuts to help them survive the winter. Typical of those birds that do remain in cool – or cold – temperate climates and rely almost entirely on an insectivorous diet would be the Treecreeper. Soft-plumaged and mouse-like as it creeps upward in spirals around tree trunks, the Treecreeper when seen at close quarters has what could be described as a rather 'bad-tempered' expression. Its slim beak is long and down-curved, producing a 'scowl', and its large eyes are sheltered beneath overhanging eyebrows accentuated by a pale eyestripe set in a permanent 'frown'.

Many insect eaters have a slender, pointed beak, which makes picking up their prey relatively easy. The length and the curve of the Treecreeper's beak may well enable it to probe into crevices too deep or too concealed for other birds seeking the hidden eggs or larvae of overwintering arthropods. It seems likely that the relatively large eyes of the Treecreeper, and the beetling eyebrows, are an adaptation to hunting in these surrounds: the woodland is gloomy enough in midwinter, and to find tiny concealed food items deep in the crevices of the bark must demand eyesight comparable to that of the owls. It would be interesting to know if the retina of the Treecreeper's eye is, like that of the owls, particularly rich in those sensory cells called rods that confer particularly good poor-light vision (see Chapter 3).

Most predominantly insectivorous birds, however, are migrants, summer visitors to temperate climates relying on their powers of navigation and flight endurance to escape the hazards of overwintering too far north. There are many examples: the warbler family, for example, where though the vast majority like the Willow Warbler and Whitethroat migrate, some – the Dartford Warbler of heathland and Cetti's Warbler from swampy areas – have developed the skills necessary to overwinter and are sedentary, even surviving most winters in Britain with little evident problem so far as populations are concerned.

More extremely adapted is the Swift – aerial for much of its relatively long life, drinking, mating and feeding on the wing – whose extraordinary strategy for nestling survival over hard times is described in Chapter 5. Another example of extreme adaptation is the Spotted Flycatcher. Here the beak structure differs from the finely pointed, delicate structure of the warblers, being more akin to that of the Swift. The mouth gapes open almost literally from ear to ear and is surrounded at the base by stiff bristles, all designed to maximize its catching area when insects are hunted on the wing (the Nightjar, too, shares this adaptation).

The Spotted Flycatcher, so familiar in woodland and in gardens, has also a well-developed feeding behaviour pattern to augment this catching capacity. It chooses an exposed perch offering good vantage in all directions, and sits and waits for an appropriate insect to fly into view. Prey sighted, the Flycatcher darts off to catch it – often with a 'snap' audible some distance away – before returning, frequently to the same perch, to resume its vigilance. Sometimes the prey secured in such flight is substantial, a moth, butterfly or beetle; but sometimes it may be an insect as small as an aphid. Bearing in mind that a considerable part of an insect is going to be its chitinous exoskeleton, hard and indigestible to any bird, it becomes difficult to see how a flight of several metres, just to secure a tiny prey item, can possibly be effective in the sense of energy conservation: it would seem unlikely that an aphid could supply even the energy to 'fuel' the flight to catch it, let alone contribute to the hour-to-hour 'running-cost' energy demands of keeping the bird warm and alive.

The shrike family, considered as a whole, is probably better classified as insectivorous than anything else, though most species also eat small amphibians, reptiles, birds and mammals. Interestingly, the shrike beak is closely similar in shape to that of the birds of prey – short and sharply hooked – and as it has an additional notch near the tip, is even more effective at holding prey, especially insects like beetles which are difficult to grasp. Perhaps the crucial difference is that with the shrikes it is normally the *beak* that is the main feeding tool or weapon, hence this extra embellishment.

Shrikes, too, show an interesting adaptive behaviour when it comes to storing their prey. Once widespread in south-eastern Britain, the Red-backed Shrike was colloquially known there as the 'butcher bird' because of its habit of impaling surplus prey on the thorns of a gorse or hawthorn bush for later consumption. In Europe and Africa this and other shrikes have kept up with the times, adaptively speaking, by using the almost ubiquitous supply of barbed-wire fencing for their larders.

Other specialist insectivores must deal with noxious prey items: best-known are the bee-eaters, highly coloured, largely tropical birds, most of which hail from Africa. But one beautiful multi-coloured member is a summer visitor to southern parts of Europe, where it can be watched. Bee-eaters are not, as is sometimes supposed, immune to the venom from bees which, as their name implies, feature quite regularly in their diet They are as susceptible to bee stings as any other bird or mammal, but having caught their prey in a dazzling rainbow-like flourish of flight, they hold it carefully at the extreme tip of their rather long beak and return swiftly to a perch, there battering the unfortunate insect to death before consuming it. Once it has been safely swallowed, the Bee-eater's digestive juices rapidly dispose of the toxic properties of the venom.

Red-backed Shrike

Plant-eating birds

Rather more of the smaller birds have a diet primarily composed of various types of vegetable matter ranging from buds, through leaves and flowers, to the fruits and seeds, and, below ground, to the tuberous food-storage organs of some plants like rhizomes and stolons. A survey of plant eating must begin somewhere, and the bud in winter seems to offer a suitable starting point. Even most gardeners would agree that the Bullfinch *is* a beautiful bird, the male splendid with his scarlet breast and black cap, the female a subtler mixture of suede browns. Both sexes possess a purplish-black tail surmounted by a white rump patch, so often all we see of them as they dart away deep into the bushes.

However, let no one doubt the other side of the Bullfinch character: beneath the black cap is a sharp, slightly hooked beak, rather more rounded in profile than the typical wedge-shaped beaks of the other finches. This is ideal for nipping off whole buds from trees and shrubs and biting out the core, a process so lightning-fast that blackcurrant and gooseberry buds can be husked and devoured at the staggering rate of thirty a minute! Those of popular ornamental shrubs like forsythia go even faster.

Since the time of the first Queen Elizabeth, the Bullfinch has had a price on its head. Even in those poorly documented days fruit growers were sufficiently incensed by the havoc caused by the bird eating apple and pear fruit buds during the winter months to offer one penny reward for 'everie Bulfynche or other Byrde that devoureth the blowthe of fruit'. Many gardeners or fruit growers, surveying the wreckage after Bullfinches have been feeding – the scattered litter is painfully conspicuous on top of snow – see so many bud fragments that they assume that nothing could have been eaten and that the attack was sheer wanton vandalism. Not a bit of it: the assault is not only technically skilful, but also purposeful. Deep in the heart of the bud lies the flower initial – in a pear bud about the size of a pin-head and looking like a miniature cauliflower. Here, not surprisingly, much of the 'goodness' (in nutritional terms) of the bud is concentrated, and it is this that the Bullfinches are sensibly seeking when they discard the residue of the bud.

For all or most of the year Bullfinches eat a variety of wild natural foods. In summer they concentrate on the seeds of dandelion, buttercup and many other plants, turning to nettle, and later dock, in autumn. As winter comes, most seeds fall, but dock and bramble remain available. After Christmas, these seeds are supplemented by ash keys until, late in winter, the buds of blackthorn and hawthorn begin to swell to a worthwhile size. Many Bullfinches will survive perfectly well all their lives on this natural diet, and it seems that only when natural supplies fail will those birds resident close to gardens or orchards turn their attention to cultivated varieties. When they do, they find them such a palatable alternative that the forthcoming summer's fruit crop is almost destroyed.

The flower feeders

Rather strangely, plant flowers relatively rarely suffer attack from birds, and specialists in flower feeding are largely confined to tropical birds, the hummingbirds of the New World and the Sunbirds of the Old World. Though similar in their glittering iridescent plumage and in their hovering behaviour, these two groups are unrelated taxonomically, their similarities yet another example of the products of convergent evolution, shaping widely differing birds to the same functional goal.

Of the two it is the hummingbirds that are the more extremely evolved. Highly sophisticated flight, with a shoulder joint allowing wingbeats even in a 'figure-of-eight' format so that the bird can keep its body near-vertical yet fly forwards, backwards, or hover stationary in front of a flower, is the most striking feature. The beak also shows marked adaptation, in some cases being almost tubular, and functioning in much the same way as a drinking straw to reach the nectar source deep in a flower. Such a life style makes extremely high energy demands which the sugar-rich nectar is able to meet. Feeding is not possible at night, and many hummingbird species slow down their metabolism appreciably, with lowered body temperatures, heart beat and respiratory rates reducing them to a form of torpor, thus enabling them to survive cold nights.

Nearer home, gardeners are again outraged at the apparent vandalism shown by House Sparrows attacking plants like crocuses and primulas early in the spring. This is a time when temperatures are often low and food for the Sparrow perhaps not always easily come by. In most areas the pathways, lawns and flower beds are littered with mostly yellow flower remains, some other colours being virtually untouched. Interestingly, yellow flowers tend to be rather better supplied with nectar than other colours – perhaps as a 'reward' to the visiting pollinating insect – which are often man-produced deviants bred purely for garden colour. It is this richer nectar supply that the House Sparrows are seeking when they rip open the bases of the flowers, for to them it is a valuable food at a time of hardship.

Brassica leaves : inadequate winter diet of the Woodpigeon

Like flowers, plant leaves too seem rarely to feature in bird diets, save in the case of the grazing water fowl already discussed. Many arable farmers, thinking of the tremendous damage that Woodpigeon flocks can cause to brassica crops, would bridle at such a statement, but it remains true to the extent that, for Woodpigeons, those brassicas grown at such expense represent a very poor diet indeed, so poor that they can only just support the bird through a winter day and its subsequent night. By feeding at full speed all day, the Woodpigeon can keep alive through the daylight hours, but with little if anything in reserve to help it survive the long, even colder hours of darkness during which it cannot feed. What the pigeon can do, however, to supplement its diet is to fly to roost as late as possible, with a crop full to bursting point with brassica leaves. Watch winter Woodpigeons flighting to roost across a chill winter sunset and note how bulging are their throats: the huge bulge is the crop, crammed with plant material, which the bird steadily digests during the night hours to keep itself warm and alive.

Large-scale, really severe Woodpigeon damage to brassica crops is in fact a relatively recent problem, because the birds' prime winter food – and one on which winter survival was nowhere near so difficult – used to be clover stolons. These stolons are far more compact, more nutritious and more energy-giving than brassica leaves, which have been eaten only as a substitute since regular clover-rich leys vanished from most farms' rotations in the ever-accelerating search for more intensive land use and higher returns. Once again as Woodpigeon control by shooting or scaring – for example, with gas-fired bangers – is so ineffective, it would seem that progress on one front only produces setbacks on another.

Fruit as food

In temperate climates, when it comes to fleshy fruits like apples and pears, though birds like Starlings, Blue Tits and Blackbirds can and do cause damage to some varieties, rarely is it serious, perhaps reflecting the relatively lowly role of fruit in birds' diets in these regions. Fruit eating becomes far more commonplace in the tropics of Africa and South America where, because of both the climate and the naturally greater diversity of plant life, fruit is available in several if not many forms year-round.

Fruit presents a number of difficulties to the intending fruit eater (frugivore) – paralleled by appropriate human equivalents. For a start, the protein-to-calorie ratio is extremely low, while the watery (and not very useful) bulk is very large. In addition there is often a bulky but always considerable indigestible mass of seed within the fruit. Intriguingly, in tropical America, studies have shown relatively little in the way of consistent morphological adaptations of the digestive tract to fruit eating, though there are important adaptations in digestive physiology.

Although frugivores of all sizes seem as a general rule to include a wide variety of fruits in their diet, the physiological adaptations seem linked to body size and to the fact that the smaller birds (like the extensive tanager family) eat mainly small, carbohydrate-rich fruit or berries, while larger birds (like the toucan family) consume a wider range of fruit sizes which embraces both the small, carbohydrate-rich types and also larger lipid- (or fat-) rich fruits. To see a toucan with its massive and unwieldy – yet not heavy – beak handling a tiny berry, picking it up delicately between the beak tips and then tossing it back deep into its throat, as a schoolboy does a sweet, is to realize just how adept at food 'handling' birds are, despite their lack of hands.

Returning to temperate climates, some birds there are able to deal with relatively large and tough fruits like acorns. Watch any oakwood in autumn: at this time of year Jays are at their most obvious, flopping away across the fields, looking unusually heavy-headed and often actually carrying an acorn in their beak as well as several in their crop. These acorns are picked up from beneath the oak or sometimes plucked off the twigs directly. Some are eaten on the spot – the Jay has a beak that is both sharp and stout, and well equipped with muscles – while others are taken away and buried, apparently at random, in nearby fields.

It is often argued that some of these will later be found by Jays – not necessarily those that cached them – but that most are likely to remain unfound and, rather than benefiting Jays, are more likely to give rise to further generations of oak trees! Jay experts, however, would disagree, suggesting that acorns are the Jay's main autumn and winter food supply, and that many of these hidden acorns are eaten in spring. At this time of year, when resources are often at their lowest ebb, such a food source would be extremely useful to 'build up' the birds for the oncoming breeding season, and sometimes stocks may last long enough to be used through into early summer to help feed the youngsters. Experimental evidence suggests that Jays find a high proportion of the acorns that they cache, being able to locate them even beneath a covering of snow.

Even so, some acorns would be dispersed to new areas to grow and potentially to expand the range of the oak. The case of the oak and the Jay is an example of an association between a plant (and its seeds) and a bird that is so closely knit it could be described as a symbiosis. Near-parallels of various sorts are legion and serve to underline the relationship of plants and birds so far as seeds are concerned. If the plant seeds rely on other means of dispersal – for example, the wind in the case of thistledown – in an evolutionary adaptive sense the plant takes steps to defend its seeds – in the case of the thistle with prickles impenetrable to all but the specialist Goldfinch. If, on the other hand, the plant is relying on a bird to disperse its seeds, most commonly via the digestive tract, it is to be expected that the plant will offer the fleshy coat of its seed to the bird as a sort of bait 'reward'. This fleshy covering may be nutritious and is often also brightly coloured as, for example, in deep-red hawthorn berries or bright-orange rosehips, each tempting members of the thrush family.

The finches: built for seed eating

Nowhere are the subtle differences in beak adaptation better arranged for understanding than in the various finches. The smaller species, like the Siskin and Redpoll, have diminutive beaks to carry small seeds. These are often collected on the ground, but both these birds have a tit-like agility that allows them to hang acrobatically from alder or birch cones still on the tree and extract the seeds *in situ*. Linnet and Greenfinch beaks are stouter, and able to handle larger food items, even sunflower seeds in the case of the Greenfinch.

At the top of this ascending scale is the handsome Hawfinch, almost

Top row from left: Goldfinch, Redpoll Bullfinch; bottom row from left: Hawfinch, Greenfinch, Crossbill

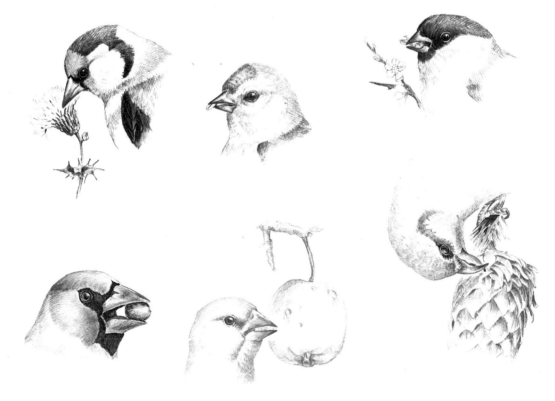

as large as a thrush and with a massive pyramidal beak almost 2cm (about ¾in) long, wide and deep. On the palate of the Hawfinch are ridges and grooves that allow food items like cherry, plum and sloe stones to be held firmly, while the apparently oversize head is that way because it houses the powerful jaw muscles necessary to crush such items. What the Hawfinch seeks is the kernel within the stone which is highly nutritious, and the crushing force that the jaws can exert to obtain their food has been measured at a staggering 160lbs per square inch!

Then there are the specialists. The Bullfinch has already received mention, but most obvious is the Crossbill, a bird of conifer woodland and often dependent on the seeds within fir cones for food. These it extracts with its parrot-like beak with crossed tips, slipping it sideways into the gaps in the woody cone and dextrously pulling out the seed.

Hawfinch
jaw muscles

Less obvious as a specialist is the Goldfinch. Its beak is long for a finch – and with tweezer-like skill allows the seeds of prickly plants like teazels and thistles to be extracted with impunity. Hence the autumn spectacle of flocks (or 'charms') of Goldfinches bejewelling the seed heads of plants that other birds cannot tackle.

The locust-like *Quelea*

Some seed-eating birds are remarkably abundant. Much discussion has centred on which is the world's most numerous bird and sea birds like the Little Auk and Wilson's Petrel – both of which nest in remote, almost inaccessible regions – have often been suggested as leading contenders for this title. Estimates put their populations in the order of tens of millions, but even such vast figures pale to insignificance in comparison with one of the tropical and sub-tropical African weaver birds, related to the finches and, like them, a seed eater. The same bird, perhaps not totally unexpectedly, happens also to be the most damaging avian agricultural pest on a world scale: it is the Black-faced Dioch, often known by its scientific name *Quelea*.

Quelea occur in enormous flocks, looking astonishingly like the swarms of locusts that strike dread into the hearts of subsistence farmers of arid parts of Africa. They feed, breed and roost gregariously, and range over much of south and central Africa. *Quelea* damage various cereal crops, particularly guinea corn, both by eating the grains and in causing 'physical' damage by the sheer weight of numbers in the flocks. Cultivated cereals seem not to be preferred foods; smaller seeds of various wild grasses form the bulk of the diet. Even in years of severe damage, only twenty per cent of *Quelea* food intake may be of cultivated cereals.

The widespread and vast areas producing wild seed in the rainy seasons are exploited by many animals, but it is only towards the end of dry seasons that food shortage forces *Quelea* flocks into the river valleys and inundation zones favoured for agricultural crops. The 'last straw' comes at the onset of the rains, when any remaining seeds promptly germinate and the *Quelea* flocks face starvation. This provokes a merging of already-large flocks and causes nomadic migrations in search of areas where earlier rains have replenished seed stocks, both wild and cultivated. On these the vast and ravenously destructive hordes descend – to such effect that in South Africa damage was devastating in one year despite the poisoning of an estimated 100 million *Quelea* by aerial sprays. Despite this massive slaughter, carried out under very difficult conditions, as *Quelea* range over several million square kilometres in areas where communications are poor in the extreme, the population level appeared little affected. Surely the ability to withstand such an onslaught and emerge as buoyant as ever must make the *Quelea* the most numerous bird.

Omnivorous birds: the gulls

Reference has already been made several times to various birds with a fairly wide flexibility in their diet. The most adaptable in this respect should perhaps properly be described as omnivores – eating just about anything that comes their way. Immediate examples come to mind –

the crow family, for example. Take the Jay, which despite its close association with the oak and its acorns, will eat any available carrion it can find, regularly pillages small bird nests in spring and summer, eating the eggs and young with evident relish, and which readily turns its beak in autumn to berries and even to ripe apples and pears.

Perhaps most typical of this class of avian feeders, and certainly in Europe the most successful bird family of our century if sheer increase in numbers is the main criterion, are the gulls. In Victorian times and earlier, gulls – take the Herring Gull and the Black-headed Gull as well-known examples – ventured inland only rarely : hence the term 'seagull' and hence also the various old sayings relating sightings of gulls inland to stormy conditions at sea. At the turn of the century the Black-headed Gull was a rarity in London; today, however, it is one of the city's most numerous birds, feeding from the hand in city squares almost as often as do the ubiquitous feral pigeons.

Gulls of several species, roosting in safety on the wide expanses of urban parks and playing fields, are a commonplace sight year-round, and it would be difficult to conceive a day spent birdwatching anywhere in Britain, at any time of year, when no single gull was seen. Today the Common Gull feeds on wet winter pastures; Black-headed Gulls follow the plough just like Rooks have always done; and even on the tops of mountains, like Snowdon in North Wales, Herring Gulls are about, scavenging the left-over sandwiches from climbers' and hill-walkers' lunches.

Scavenging appears to be the key to the gulls' success. Basically fish and mollusc eaters, they had an intrinsic omnivorous nature that encouraged feeding on carcases and on fish offal both beside trawlers at sea and in close proximity with man in the fishing ports scattered round our coasts. From Victorian times not only has mankind in Western Europe become better fed and more affluent in general, he has also become far more conscious of hygiene. Thus doubtfully wholesome food is disposed of – not, as in the old days, to a midden or compost heap in each garden, but to the much larger refuse tip associated with each community or group of communities.

In recent years by far the best place for the birdwatcher to get a good view of various gulls was the nearest rubbish dump, *not* the coast. Only now are health considerations causing the local authorities to cover refuse with earth as soon as possible after it has been tipped, but even so the gulls are so expert that most obtain a meal before it can be concealed. Food obtainable at such a source may largely be in the nature of domestic scraps, but occasionally larger quantities of fish, meat or poultry offal may be dumped, or indeed fruit or grain, all of which is avidly consumed.

Offered such a bounteous food source, the numbers of some gulls – especially Black-headed, Herring and to an extent Lesser Black-backed – have risen dramatically. In recent years a continuing growth of over ten per cent per annum has been reported for many Herring Gull colonies, and the Black-headed Gull, close to extinction (unbelievable as that now seems) in Britain in the nineteenth century, had an estimated breeding population of between 150,000 and 300,000 pairs in 1972, a number which would be greatly augmented each year by winter visitors from the Continent. Not only has this rate of growth allowed the gulls to spread to almost all habitats, in the case of the Herring Gull in particular it has put extreme pressures on other less dominant sea birds breeding in their ancestral coastal areas. As a result conservation organizations are seriously concerned over the likely extinction of some tern colonies, and have instituted regular culls of the breeding gulls in order to allow the terns room and some freedom from otherwise almost continuous harassment.

Changing diet with the season

Into a rather more natural omnivorous category fall several very familiar garden birds like the Robin and the Blackbird. Among smaller birds an omnivorous diet is indicated by beak shape, typified by the medium-length, moderately robust, fairly pointed beak of the Blackbird. It is easy to watch how effective this beak is at dealing with food as diverse as worms on the lawn, soft apples on the tree and bread crusts on the bird table. Though there may be seasonal shifts in emphasis, such as that created by the availability of fruit primarily in late summer and autumn, such birds are opportunist and are able to eat whatever is available – flesh or fruit. Thus, though it may be 'out of season', surplus or poor-quality fruit disposed of from farm cold stores in spring is quickly taken advantage of by Blackbirds, and they are always ready to tackle novel 'prey' items which, for this species, are on record as including small frogs, lizards, goldfish, and even a fair-sized slow worm! Though the warblers are generally regarded as insectivorous, that term should be qualified by 'largely' as, towards the end of their summer stay in temperate Europe, their diet changes dramatically. From virtually purely insect food, as the time approaches for them to 'fuel-up' for the long journey south, the warblers turn increasingly to late-summer and autumn fruit, like elderberries and blackberries. Though high in fluid content, these are eaten in great quantity and processed quickly through the bird's digestive tract, which allows the sugar to be readily assimilated and converted into fats. These fats are stored around the organs within the body cavity, beneath the skin and even, in extreme cases, beneath the eyelids.

Perhaps the best example of a warbler which changes its diet is the Sedge Warbler, often to be found in open woodland and scrub in late summer seeking fruit. As a long-haul migrant it may *double* in weight in the last few weeks of its residence in the north! Ringing studies have revealed the magnitude of this weight increase, and compared with their slim summer selves, the birds appear almost spherical and have difficulty in making height with any speed on release from the hand. Recoveries of ringed birds, coupled with calculations on their levels of stored energy and the rate of its use in flight, indicate that Sedge Warblers from southern Britain may, by this feeding change, be able routinely to accumulate sufficient energy reserves to fly to Africa – even perhaps to overfly the Sahara Desert – in a single non-stop journey. This is a prodigious performance for a creature which, even at its maximum, weighs considerably less than an old-fashioned ounce (28g)!

Resident birds may put fruit to a rather different use. In the migrants there is a sharp increase in weight in late summer, whereas the resident species (Robin, Dunnock, Blackbird, for example) increase in weight to a rather smaller degree – ten to thirty per cent – and appreciably later. The purpose of this early-winter weight increase, again due to stored fatty materials, is not to fuel journeys but more to provide a sub-cutaneous layer of fat that serves as effective insulation. At the same time it acts as an energy reserve that can be metabolically mobilized at times of severe stress – for example, to help provide life-giving warmth overnight at times when temperatures are very low and when poor weather further limits feeding opportunities already restricted by short day-lengths.

Blue Tit

A meal at man's expense

Among the omnivores more than in any other group of birds are the benefits and the techniques of feeding versatility best demonstrated. The garden-living Blue Tit, not content with scraps, fat and peanuts on the bird table, often 'bites the hand that feeds it' by attacking milk bottles, puncturing the tops and drinking as much of the cream as it can reach. This habit developed in a very small way in the 1930s, when milk bottles were tall and had card caps. It spread rapidly, to become almost national within a decade, and the Blue Tit technique was robust enough to withstand the changes to squat bottles and to aluminium-foil caps. For many years, though, it seemed that

doorstep-delivered milk packaged in waxed cardboard containers was impregnable to tit attack, but now in some areas tits have discovered the means of obtaining entry to these cartons too by persistently pecking and thus puncturing one corner!

Not only do most urban milkmen deliver milk, but also eggs. The bird with the most evil reputation for egg taking is without question the Magpie. This bird – as a member of the crow family, duly cautious in its actions – has recently expanded considerably, particularly colonizing urban areas both for feeding and for breeding. Many trees, even in some inner-city squares in northern Britain, now hold characteristically bulky, spherical Magpie nests. Most Magpie feeding in urban areas is carried out soon after first light and thus is often unobserved and in consequence its real frequency is not realized. In 1975 came the first report, inevitably followed by others, of attacks by Magpies on eggs in cartons, both plastic and cardboard, left by milkmen who now, besides covering the milk against marauding tits, must protect the eggs with an upturned flower pot!

Extremely specialist feeders

Having reviewed a series of examples of bird diets and feeding techniques, and seen how they are linked to the birds' life styles, group by group, it is appropriate to look in a little detail at some of the more extreme specialists. High in the mountains of the more arid parts of Europe, Africa and Asia lives the Lammergeyer, or Bearded Vulture – distantly related to the Old World vultures and sharing their habit of feeding from the remains of carcases. However, Lammergeyers are everywhere few in number and are rarely dominant among the unseemly scrum of vultures surrounding a freshly found carcase. Though they will take flesh given the opportunity, more often they needs must wait until the other vultures have gorged their fill, and little but bones remain.

This is where the Lammergeyer's specialist feeding technique comes into its own. Though apparently hardly nutritious, the larger bones of the carcase do contain substantial quantities of marrow – but these, especially the long bones of the legs, are too substantial to be eaten whole. The Lammergeyer therefore picks them up in its feet and flies above a suitably rocky area before dropping them, if necessary time and again, until they break. Then the bird uses its long, slim tongue, shaped like a narrow trowel, to scoop the marrow from the core of the bone. In fact the tongue precisely parallels in shape the marrow scoops – usually made of silver – of the last century, used to extract marrow from the long bones at a time when, to humans, bone marrow was a table delicacy. Other fragments of bone, with marrow attached, may be eaten whole. No matter how sharp and dangerous they seem, powerfully acidic digestive juices soon break them down.

Avian tool users

Another of the Old World's 'necrophagous' birds, the Egyptian Vulture, also achieves distinction in this specialist category as one of the world's few avian tool users. Considering the feeding difficulties birds face having forfeited their hands for flight, it is more than a little remarkable that the use of artificial feeding aids, or tools, is not far more widespread. Though carcase feeding for much of the time like its relatives, the Egyptian Vulture has a scavenger's taste for Ostrich eggs. These are huge and thick-shelled, while the Egyptian is among the smaller and weaker-beaked vultures. None the less some (though not all) Egyptian Vultures have found a solution: they walk about in search of a suitably sized, liftable piece of rock, and with this held in their mouths they strike at the egg – often many times – until it cracks open to offer them a huge meal.

Also using a feeding aid is the Carmine Bee-eater from Africa. It favours feeding on large grassland insects and may be seen riding perched on the back of a goat grazing in arid grassland, making the occasional hunting sally from this mobile vantage point to secure prey disturbed into flight by the passing feet of its mount. Perhaps more remarkably, some Carmine Bee-eaters will 'hitch a lift' on the back of one of the larger African plains birds, the Kori Bustard, which prowls on foot through the grasslands, disturbing flying insects for the Bee-eater while seeking its own food of lizards, snakes and large insects actually on the ground.

Just south of the Equator, in the Pacific Ocean off the coast of Equador, lie the Galapagos Islands made famous by Charles Darwin in his researches leading to the publication of his evolutionary theories in *The Origin of Species*. The avifauna of these islands is unusual, with several unique birds of which possibly the best-known are grouped as 'Darwin's Finches'. One of these, perhaps contrary to expectations arising from its name, is also a tool user: the Woodpecker Finch. Rather than hammering its way into timber to extract wood-boring insect larvae, this bird is reported on occasion to break off a spine from a nearby pricky pear cactus and to use this spine as a sort of spear, as we might use a pin to extract a winkle from its shell. Holding the spine in its beak, the Woodpecker Finch probes likely holes until it encounters a larva that it can stab and withdraw to be eaten.

Versatility in the woodpecker family

Though they are not tool users, no less amazing are the feeding tactics of the woodpecker family. In North America some woodpeckers – called Sapsuckers – drill into the tree slightly up-tilted holes, into which sugar-rich sap dribbles to collect and later be drunk. A human parallel might be the Malaysian rubber grower who taps tree trunks to collect the latex from which the rubber is made. Still in North America another woodpecker – the Acorn Woodpecker – selects a suitably soft trunk, often birch, in which it and others of its group excavate holes where collected acorns are lodged to serve as a food store for the birds during the oncoming winter months.

Just as remarkable are the familiar European woodpeckers, the Green and the Great Spotted. Most woodpeckers have extremely long tongues – that of the Green Woodpecker can be protruded for several centimetres. This tongue is supported by two long, very slim and flexible bones, the hyoids, and when not in use obviously presents a potential storage problem in a bird with a beak only 4 or 5cm ($1\frac{1}{2}$–2ins) long.

Great Spotted
Woodpecker tongue

This difficulty is overcome by use of a special storage tube into which the tongue recoils, passing along the underside of the lower jaw and down the sides of the neck for some distance before looping up the back of the neck, finishing on top of the skull.

The Green Woodpecker, more often than not, feeds on the ground, usually seeking ants and their larvae. Having excavated an entrance to the ants' nest, the bird extends its tongue covered in frothy, sticky saliva along the ant runs, trapping on it ants and 'ants eggs' (the pupae in their cases) which it then swallows. Though its tongue is, relatively speaking, much the same length, the Great Spotted Woodpecker uses a different approach. Having hacked its way into the timber, employing its beak like a combination of hammer and chisel and twisting its head to prise off flakes of wood, the Great Spotted uses its tongue like a harpoon. The tip is horny and has backward-pointing barbs – just like a whaler's harpoon in miniature – and it is poked along the wood-boring insect's tunnel until the larva is encountered, stabbed and withdrawn on the barbed tip to be eaten. Headaches, incidentally, are prevented by a shock-absorbing pad of cartilaginous tissue between the wood-pecker's beak and skull!

Woodpecker adaptations do not stop at the head, either. The central tail-feather shafts are specially strengthened, and serve as a prop while the bird works upright on the trunk – rather like a built-in shooting stick. The feet, too, are different: long sharp claws are predictable, but the toes are arranged two forwards, two back, to give maximum grip at all times on the bark. In most other birds the arrangement is three toes forward and one back.

How birds drink

Drinking is an essential part of eating in the broad sense and is a function that birds may find difficult. Swallows and Swifts skim a pond surface, beak open, to obtain their water requirements, while most small birds dip their beaks like a spoon, then raise the head to let the water trickle into the throat. None can lap up water with the tongue like, say, a dog or cat, and only relatively few, such as the Woodpigeon, can place their beaks in the water and drink for an uninterrupted period as if through a straw.

Some desert birds, like the Budgerigar, may obtain most of the water they need from the seeds they eat – no matter how dry these seem – but it is the way in which other desert-breeding birds provide water for their young that is particularly fascinating. Some of the sand grouse may nest many kilometres from the nearest water hole: fast-flying and

pigeon-like, they may flight there, morning and evening, in flocks to drink. It is after he has drunk his fill that the male wades into the shallows with fluffed-up belly feathers. Such is their structure that they soak up water like a sponge and, when fully saturated, he flies back to the nest. There, standing over the young, he waits for them to quench their thirst by pushing their beaks up into his belly feathers and sucking out the moisture.

As a final example, we can look behind what must be considered as one of the seven ornithological wonders of the modern world, the amazing gathering, often millions strong, of the bright carmine-pink Lesser Flamingos on Lake Nakuru, one of the alkaline lakes of the Rift Valley in Kenya. Leaving aside the thrill of the sheer spectacle and the aesthetic delights of the sight, particularly in misty early-morning light, there is much to marvel at in the biology and ecology of the birds in that strange location. The murky waters, rich in soda, are sufficiently alkaline to sting a grazed human hand immersed in them, yet the Lesser Flamingos plunge in their heads – almost upside down in true *Alice in Wonderland* fashion – submerging mouth, nostrils and even eyes in the process.

The cloudiness of the water derives from the presence of countless millions of microscopic, single-celled, blue-green algae that also can flourish, with scant competition, in these alkaline conditions. It is on these minute plants that the Flamingos, each standing more than 1m ($3\frac{1}{4}$ft) tall, feed with relish and evident success, though it is difficult to conceive how they manage to gather enough of such small food items sufficiently quickly to keep well fed. The secret lies in the very complex structure of the banana-shaped beak, much of which is composed of fine lamellae (horny plates) arranged something like the whalebone in baleen whales and serving the same filtering function. The thick fleshy tongue, lying, close-fitting, in a groove in the mandible, is drawn back to suck water and algae in, then pushed forward, cycle-pump-like, to expel the water while the algae are retained on the filters to be swallowed. This picturesque spectacle is indicative at the one time of both the huge range of adaptations used by birds feeding and their fascination to the birdwatcher.

5 The Breeding Season

Way back in palaeontological time, perhaps 140 or 150 million years ago or even more, prototype birds began to develop from the then dominant reptile stock. Though the fossil record could helpfully have been rather more clear (see Chapter 1), there can be no real doubt of the reptilian ancestry of today's birds, or mammals for that matter. The mammals, too, developed as an offshoot from the reptiles, but the birds – unlike the true mammals – have retained the egg, on a reptilian pattern, as the means of reproduction and as a protective capsule for the fertilized ovum as it develops through to hatching.

Clearly, as the method has endured so well over so many millions of years, there can be no doubt that the egg should be considered highly successful in evolutionary terms. Not only that, but the reptiles which exist today also still use the technique, though often reptilian eggshells are flexible and parchment-like rather than rigidly calcified as are the birds'.

Although flight itself is by no means unique to birds, in them it has evolved to such a degree, and has been adaptively exploited so widely, that in many ways it should perhaps be considered as their most important feature. This ability to fly effectively, with high manoeuvrability and allowing ample scope for the diverse lives that the various species live, has inevitably brought with it a number of constraints to bird anatomy. The need for lightness with strength is one of the more obvious of these, and familiar to modern aeronautical engineers. What is true for the permanent bones of the skeleton is equally true of the temporary developing offspring.

Imagine the difficulties for a female bird, burdened for a considerable period – weeks if not months – with a slowly maturing foetus, or, more likely, group of foetuses of mammalian type, remorselessly increasing in weight until she gives birth. For a start, her skeletal structure (with its rigid 'box' protecting the vital organs) would be ill-adapted to carry and protect the load. The demands on respiration, blood supply and energy to fly with this burden would be almost impossible to meet. Also, as with heavily pregnant mammals, when the female's ability to escape danger is severely restricted, the risks of high predation at a critical time – particularly critical so far as population dynamics are concerned – would outweigh any benefits.

Eggs have the advantage

The contrast between the mammalian system of reproduction and that of the birds, in which a series of eggs is each rapidly produced within a protective shell, then quickly laid before the next egg in the chain is of burdensome proportions, is dramatic. In addition the egg is normally laid within a protective nest and then incubated, to some degree at will, by the parents which remain free to fly to save their own lives in the face of extreme danger. This would seem to be a most effective evolutionary strategy to solve the problem of the burden attached to foetal care, but of course it too has its problems. Though they are protected to a degree, it remains true – and obvious even to the casual observer of the fate of nests in a garden – that levels of egg loss as a result of climate and predators are astronomical seen through human eyes.

There can be no simple judgement on whether the techniques of reproduction using eggs, as variously evolved by birds, are 'better' or

Ostrich pair at nest

'worse' than the mammalian pattern, based as it is on the foetus developing full-term within the mother. Indeed, there are even compromises, the most obvious being in the marsupials where much of the foetal development occurs within the pouch (say, of a kangaroo), from which in dire emergency a youngster of any age can quickly be ejected if it becomes necessary to save the mother's skin. Each approach has its apparent advantages, and its hazards, but each has been tailored by evolution and adaptation to be as effective as is possible for its own particular purpose.

Variations in egg size

Consider first the eggs themselves. With the great range of bird sizes, from hummingbirds little bigger than a bee to ostriches standing much taller than a man, a great deal of variation in the size of the egg is inevitable. What is more interesting is that the logical expectation of a simple relationship of egg size to body size is not borne out: the relationship is far from simple. One reason for this is that some birds lay but a single egg in their clutch, while others either lay many – fifteen is not uncommon – in a single clutch or produce several clutches each season, each of several eggs.

Hummingbird nest

However, there is another broadly defined reason: that the smaller species on the whole lay proportionately larger eggs. For example, the Blue Tit – normally producing one and sometimes two clutches of eight to fifteen eggs – lays an egg about 1cm ($\frac{1}{3}$in.) long, weighing just over $\frac{1}{2}$ gram. This amounts to roughly five or six per cent of the female's body weight. Right at the other end of the size scale, the Ostrich – which also lays a clutch of eggs often into double figures – produces a gigantic 2.5-litre- (4-pint)-capacity egg, weighing about 1400 grams – but this represents only some one per cent of her body weight.

The purpose of shell colour

In many ways the most striking feature of birds' eggs, at least initially, is their enormous range of colours. This is particularly apparent when large numbers of clutches of various species are seen on display in museum collections. In some cases the colours and patterns have a clear purpose. The eggs of many of the species of wading birds are a case in point: the Ringed Plover, for example, lays eggs with rather rectangular, blackish spots speckled over a sandy-coloured background, which are ideally camouflaged for the bird's typical nesting site on a sandy beach with plentiful flecks of dark seaweed and broken shell among the grains of sand.

Ringed Plover nest and eggs

In other cases the very opposite of camouflage seems intended. The Dunnock is an inconspicuous bird whose plumage – a tweed-like mixture of browns, greys, black and fawn – tends to make it merge into the background and is thus especially protective of the immobile incubating bird sitting low in a nest of dried grass and itself well concealed among dead grass or bracken. Should the female be disturbed, though, by the too-close approach of a potential predator, the eggs that she uncovers are the brightest sky-blue and almost painfully conspicuous against the dark background of the nest. This must render them unusually vulnerable to predators like magpies and jays.

Many of the hole-nesting birds – and the range is wide, from owls and woodpeckers to ducks like the Goosander, the Kingfisher, Stock Dove and Swift – seem to lay white or whitish eggs. It is thought that one reason for the pale colour is that it may help the returning bird to locate her eggs in the sudden gloom as she enters the nest chamber from the brightness of the daylight outside. Birds like owls and especially woodpeckers have long, sharp talons or claws, which could very easily penetrate the shell if clumsily placed – and thus kill the developing embryo within.

In the crowded circumstances of a nesting colony, variations in background colour shade or in the degree of patterning may well help the individual returning bird recognize its egg. This would particularly apply to birds like the Guillemot, which does not have a true nest but lays its single egg more or less side by side with those of its fellows on sea cliff ledges or rock stack tops. In other birds, however – the Tree Pipit and the Red-backed Shrike being perhaps among the best examples – the wide range of egg base colours exhibited within each species is rather more difficult to explain, as each is highly territorial by nature and there is no possibility of neighbouring nests bearing potentially confusing contents.

Sadly, this variation was, in Victorian and Edwardian times, of great attraction to collectors seeking the greatest range of colours to adorn the drawers of their egg cabinets. The dreadful toll taken by egg collectors over the years must have been a major factor in the decline of the once-common Red-backed Shrike to its current near-extinct status in Britain. Today, of course, stealing the eggs of a wild bird is illegal, though it is still practised by the unenlightened few.

The colour pigments are added to the shell after the egg has formed and its shell has been secreted, and as the egg is passing down the oviduct. The commonest ground colours are greys, blues and greens; the commonest markings, various shades of lavender and brown or black. Many of the pigments are derived from bodily waste products, for example from broken-down 'used' blood corpuscles, a most efficient alternative way of disposing of unwanted material. The spots and tadpole-like squiggles that are a feature of so many eggs are added from special secretory cells in the oviduct wall. They too are commonly formed from pigments extracted from waste products, and their shape depends very much on the movements of the egg within the oviduct, much as moving the toothbrush can create tadpole-like patterns as toothpaste is squeezed out on to the bristles.

Egg shapes and their advantages

Egg shapes, too, vary very considerably. The eggs of many birds, particularly the song and perching species – the 'everyday' tits, thrushes, finches and so on – of the order Passeriformes, are merely variations in size on the well-known general pattern of the chicken's egg. There is a strong trend among those birds whose eggs rest safe in a hole – in a tree or bank of earth, or a cavity in a building – not only to lay white eggs but also for the eggs to be almost spherical. The range of families involved is considerable, from woodpeckers, the Swift, Kingfisher and Bee-eater, to owls, some doves and the Sand Martin. Within the Passeriformes, though, there are many exceptions to this general rule, notably among the hole-nesting species of tits, flycatchers and wagtails, which retain the 'normal' shape.

Most waders – in contrast to their reasonably close relatives, the gulls – lay strikingly straight-sided eggs, pointed at one end. Very often these birds seem to produce clutches of four eggs with little individual variation, and four such pointed eggs nestle together very compactly within the nest. Wader eggs are relatively large, too, so such a neat arrangement would naturally make it easier for the incubating bird to cover and warm them efficiently. Another reason for the egg's relatively large size is so that it enables the chick inside to reach a sufficiently advanced stage at the time of hatching to get up and run within hours. To move fast at such an age demands precocious development of the legs – hence the almost grotesquely 'leggy' appearance of very young wader chicks – and these well-developed lower limbs are folded into the pointed end of the egg: an extremely efficient usage of space.

Young Redshank (left) and Blackbird (right)

In other birds it may be that habits and anatomy have combined, in evolution, also to shape the egg. For example, the divers, slim and very elongated of body for good underwater streamlining, lay distinctively long, almost sausage-shaped eggs. Another example is the Guillemot, whose single large egg is shaped like a pear, or rather better perhaps – because it is relatively straight-sided – like a child's top. On land Guillemots are clumsy birds and, as has already been explained, they often lay on narrow ledges, high above the sea. If the bird's egg is accidentally kicked or knocked, its conical shape helps to prevent it from plunging to disaster by causing it to roll in a tight circle only a few centimetres in diameter, centred on its pointed end, and in most cases the ledge is wide enough to accommodate such movement. Perhaps correctly, the Guillemot egg has been described as one of *the* masterpieces of 'evolutionary engineering'.

Guillemots

Establishing a territory

For an overview of the complete reproductive cycle in birds, the time when territories are being established makes a convenient starting point. For the majority of small birds the winter is a period of hardship, when generally low temperatures, short days (for feeding) and long nights (which must be survived) combine to make life difficult – even extremely difficult if heavy snowfall occurs. At this time they do many things communally, although not in the sense that they deliberately 'help each other out'. Communal feeding helps to exploit food resources to the full, and communal roosting aids in the conservation of energy.

As the days lengthen with the onset of spring and the temperature rises, the birds' hormone secretions change, causing striking alterations in their behaviour patterns. In the Robin, human eyes find the sexes visually difficult – probably impossible – to distinguish during the winter, and even the bird ringer, with the benefit of the bird in the hand, has no particular advantage when it comes to identifying male and female. In winter each sex tends to maintain a feeding territory and to react aggressively to any other Robin. At this time both sexes produce the fragile, high-pitched, winter song and each reacts with sharp, scolding calls and threatening postures to any other bird of the same species – though there may be areas of 'no man's land' around man-introduced artifacts like bird-feeding tables, where no one bird holds absolute rights.

As spring advances, the male retains his aggressive manner and develops his full, richer song, but the female becomes more cautious and subdued and much less ready to defend any territorial aspirations she might have had earlier. This more submissive reaction on her part leads, over some weeks and not without its temporary upsets, in the first place to her acceptance, without hostile reaction, in what has enlarged to become the basis of the male's breeding territory. Ultimately, following ritualized patterns of song and display, will occur the formation of a strong pair bond and mating.

Dazzling feathers *and* a fine voice

More strikingly to be seen in birds than in any other group of animals is a wide – even dazzling – array of plumage colours which are coupled to an extraordinarily well-developed voice production. This has given rise to an array of displays that ranges from the frenzied upside-down cascade of noise and dazzling filamentous plumes that characterize the birds of paradise in New Guinea (Vanwatu) to the simple bowing and chirruping, with shivering wings, so familiar between male and female House Sparrow. The comparatively drab House Sparrow with this evidently undistinguished performance is so successful a bird as to give the lie to any idea that either superlative song or rainbow coloration necessarily determine whether one species is better at courtship than another.

For the male, tempting and retaining a mate and the protection of the territory are of paramount importance. That this may involve an element of personal risk is well demonstrated by the various widow birds of Africa. At the start of the breeding season, the dominant male in a group – composed of a few males and several females – will moult from Corn Bunting-like insignificance into a colourful bird with a number of broad, elongated, flowing tail feathers. Clad in this breeding plumage, he will display and mate with several of the females, establishing them on nests around his bush-studded grassland territory. But his finery is not without disadvantages: African plains are rich in hawks and falcons, and his conspicuous display and copious tail, which slows down his flight speed considerably, make him an easy target. Often the prime male is killed, but then a subsidiary male, second in the dominance order, moults swiftly into breeding plumage for his period as the head of the clan: his life, too, may be a short one, so perhaps there is need to look no further for the origin of the name 'widow bird'!

The power of song

Spring and summer are also the seasons when the song birds exploit their powers to the full – though great care must be taken not to restrict that definition simply to those producing melodies attractive to human ears. Beautiful to us the voices of the Nightingale, Garden Warbler and Blackbird undeniably are, but even the song of one of the least musical of birds to human ears, the Corn Bunting, is packed with information to others of the same species. Avian hearing, like avian sight, is several times more acute than its human equivalent, and for humans to gain even a rough idea of the Corn Bunting's 'song' it is necessary to play a recording at one-quarter – or, better, one-eighth – of normal speed. The transformation is dramatic – as it is for many other species besides the Corn Bunting – with an abundance of brief notes of widely varied frequency whose qualities are lost to human ears when heard at normal speed.

It seems certain that a prime function of a bird's song is to convey messages, obviously to others of its own kind but perhaps also to different species. If this is the case, objectives like attracting a mate and establishing and 'defending' a territory (by song signposts) seem logical major uses. Regularly used song posts are the normal way of indicating territorial boundaries, and are best seen in those birds which choose prominent perches for this purpose – the Song Thrush and, particularly, the Lesser Whitethroat being good examples.

Breeding plumage and display

As with the voice, it is for the flurry of breeding activity in spring that plumage needs to be at its best, at least for small birds. For some of the larger ones, like the ducks, the plumage will have attained its full magnificence in midwinter, as display is at its peak well before the spring even though it continues into that season.

Though birds moult their feathers regularly – usually once each year – most smaller birds, rather strangely, do not moult into a fresh, spectacular breeding plumage. Most of them in fact moult in the late summer or autumn, usually into feathers superficially on the drab side with copious downy bases. The drabness allows for better camouflage at a time when obtaining food unhindered is of great importance, especially for birds like finches and buntings, feeding in flocks on stubble fields. The dense downy feather bases serve to provide effective insulation against winter temperatures. As the winter progresses, the normal processes of wear and tear cause some breakdown of the insulating layer, preventing overheating as the days become warmer. But, more important from the point of view of display, the ends of the feathers suffer from abrasion, and as the tips gradually wear away, so previously con-

cealed parts become visible, and it is these that have the richness of what we call the 'breeding plumage'. Thus the male Reed Bunting, an inconspicuous mixture of browns, fawns and blacks through the winter, in effect 'wears out' to become the handsome, black-hooded, white-collared bird with chestnut-shaded back that decorates the summer reed beds.

Generally speaking, the exaggerated posturing of display, often with feathers fluffed out, tail fanned or wings shivering, is by a single male on his own. Perhaps his posturing is directed at a nearby rival, though song displays may result in vocal competition at some distance with perhaps several other males. In some cases – notably the Ruff and the Blackcock, or Black Grouse – the males gather in small flocks for a communal display on a special patch of ground called a 'lek'. Here they indulge in mock combat – and, in the case of the Blackcock, in the most extraordinary vocalizations – and competitively display their plumages. In both cases the breeding plumage of the males is very striking, in marked contrast to the dowdiness of the females that creep around the fringes of the activity. It seems, though, that it is the females who ultimately select a partner but, once mating is accomplished, they move away as discreetly as they arrived to nest-build, lay, and raise their family without assistance from the male.

Fattening up the female

For the female finding a suitable mate and being fertilized are obviously of prime importance, but in addition she must aim to get into good

Blackcock 'lek'

condition, to withstand the considerable rigours of the breeding season, as early as possible. Several detailed studies of individual species support the idea that it is those good-condition, early-breeding females which frequently are more productive and raise more successful young than those less well prepared. In this process, usually at the close of winter and early in spring, the male may also play a part.

Taking the Blue Tit as an example, the production of eggs is an energy-intensive process, particularly so if, as in the case of this bird, the full clutch amounts to between ten and fifteen eggs. (The more commonplace tally for multi-brooded small birds is five or six.) A female Blue Tit may increase in body weight by about fifty per cent in the three weeks before laying starts, a colossal achievement in human terms. Much of this weight increase will be in the form of stored fats, and some will be used to produce the egg – in the case of the Blue Tit, one egg daily – the rest to help her through the first days of incubation when she will not be able to leave the nest for any length of time to feed. It seems most probable that 'courtship feeding – when the male presents an extra-juicy caterpillar or worm to his eager, wing-fluttering mate – may have an important effect on the female's ultimate physical state. Courtship feeding has in the past primarily been thought of as a behavioural gesture, part of pair-bond formation, of working to cement the relationship in much the same way as does a gift of chocolates, perfume or flowers from human husband to wife.

Problems facing would-be parent migrants

Many birds breeding in the far north face an additional hazard at this time. Most are long-haul migrants, and have journeyed up from Africa at high speed, pausing only to feed up at favoured sites – for the ducks, geese and waders, often the estuaries of Western Europe. As they near the end of their journey, this feeding must be extra-intensive, for once they set out – for example, from Scotland or Norway, heading for Greenland – they are entering an unknown climate. Arctic springs are notoriously fickle and bad weather may delay the thaw for days or even weeks. Thus the incoming migrants, which cannot delay arrival as the summer is all too short in any case, must be physically prepared for frozen water and snow-covered ground. In these circumstances, they must use their stored reserves both for day-to-day sustenance until the thaw releases local food supplies and to form eggs, which they must lay if the young are to fledge before the brief summer richness of food on the tundra is terminated by the snowstorms of oncoming winter.

*Golden Eagle
eyrie*

The importance of territory

The size, and indeed also the purpose, of the territory that so many breeding birds establish varies greatly. For some of the larger, primarily carnivorous birds like the Golden Eagle, the territory may be expected to supply the food needed by the parents and their one – or occasionally two – young. This may often be no easily achieved feature, given the harshness of both climate and terrain up in the mountains, hence the vast territory size of such species which may reach 100 square kilometres (38 square miles) or more. It is over this terrain that the eagles must hunt during the winter, when the climatic conditions are even worse, but the remarkable Ravens (frequent neighbours of the eagles) often breed at this time. Continued persecution by man over recent centuries has driven the once-lowland Raven to inhabit remote cliff coastlines or the unpeopled fastnesses of mountain and moorland.

Up in the hills the Ravens continue to exploit the food source that in all probability – and quite unjustly – is the cause of their unpopularity: these birds are carrion feeders above all else and raise their young on the afterbirth (placenta) of lambs, and on the carcases of lambs or ewes that have died naturally, during the rigours of lambing.

It is easy to see how the Raven's evil reputation was gained, for shepherds would disturb the bird from freshly dead lamb carcases and immediately jump to the wrong conclusion: research has shown that active, healthy lambs are only extremely rarely attacked. Lambing time in the hills is normally as early as elsewhere – at or before the start of spring – which implies that the Raven pair must have displayed, set up territory, built or restored a nest, laid eggs and incubated them, so that the hatch and the rearing of the nestlings coincides with the peak abundance of carrion. Hence Ravens are often to be seen sitting incubating with a layer of snow on their backs.

For many of the smaller song birds, it seems, the possession of a territory must be a considerable asset and its defence is of great importance: witness the stylized, posturing parades, sometimes going on for days, between two male Blackbirds in the garden, pacing up and down on either side of an apparently invisible territorial demarcation line. As part of his territorial display each will be puffed up to the greatest possible size, in order to make the most intimidating impression on his neighbour. Sometimes the respective females may join in and there may be some skirmishing and chasing, but only relatively rarely do feathers fly. Although the nest is normally located within this territory, it is unusual if the birds involved, and their growing brood, can obtain all their food from within the defended area.

A number of theories have been advanced, yet it is difficult to reach a clear conclusion as to the major purpose of territory ownership. The territory size demands of seemingly similar birds may differ greatly, and within a single species such factors as the nature of the habitat – which could obviously influence food availability – and the current population density of the bird concerned can be seen to have an effect. Wrens suffer high mortality in severe winters, and in the following summers defended territories – with rivals then on the ground – are large. As numbers increase, territory size diminishes, often dramatically: so much so that food availability seems not to be a major determining factor.

Additionally, there appears to be an awareness of non-aggressive intrusions on the part of the territory holder, best seen where a territory surrounds a favoured drinking pool, perhaps the only such water source in an arid area. All comers are allowed to drink, but we do not know how they signify their 'peaceful intentions'. Perhaps it is by some subtlety of flight pattern or attitude.

It is abundantly clear that self-sufficiency cannot be a factor in determining the size of the minute territory surrounding the nests of colonial sea birds like the Gannet, the auks, gulls and terns. In most such cases food is obtained by fishing in generally bountiful seas, shared with myriad other sea birds and competition normally avoided by differing choices of prey items (see Chapter 4). The critical factor here seems most likely to be the security from disturbance, pilfering of nest material and harassment – of adults and later their young – that determines the spacing of the nests at about two beak-thrusts' distance from each other!

How colonies operate

Sea-bird colonies benefit from the enhanced protection offered by so many eyes alert to predators – as indeed also do heronries and rookeries in terrestrial habitats – and from the massive mobbing reactive capability that colonial species can display in an attempt to drive off malevolent intruders. For some birds, the Arctic Tern and the Great Skua perhaps paramount among them, these abilities are legendary. Even harmless birdwatchers, or sheep or cattle, may be set about by screeching, dive-bombing attacks, psychologically intimidating enough but not infrequently pressed home to the point of physical contact and actual blood-letting.

Equally, the birds in these colonies may derive benefit from a simple form of information communication: many birds are seeking food over a wide area, which increases chances of success, and less successful birds may benefit from following those feeding well. That said, colonies are not peaceful places: squabbles are rife, pilfering from unattended nests commonplace, and woe betide the bird – especially one clumsy on land like the Gannet – that fails to make an accurate touch down and must run the beak-stabbing gauntlet of hostile neighbours to struggle back to its nest. In colonies of the larger gulls, aggression to straying chicks is particularly brutal, and there are numerous recorded instances of pairs – often many within a colony – feeding largely by cannibalistic attacks on the nestlings of their own kind from elsewhere in the colony.

The enormous territories of some of the larger birds, like the Golden Eagle, Peregrine and Raven, often contain several 'ancestral' nest sites which may be used in different seasons. Quite what the full range of factors is that make these sites so 'desirable', over and above nest protection, is not fully understood. Remarkably, even after a territory has lain vacant for many years, the new inhabitants have tended to select these same ancestral crags when recolonizing the area and again building nests. Such has been the case with Golden Eagles and Peregrines in Scotland where the use of certain persistent insecticides in the 1950s and early 1960s resulted, inadvertently, in the deaths of many birds of prey and dramatic reductions in the breeding success of others.

In colonial birds – like the relatively long-lived Rooks, Herons and Kittiwakes – many of the nests may survive from season to season, needing only refurbishment and perhaps some ornamentation with fresh leaves or seaweed before the eggs are laid. Generally speaking, it is the older-established pairs which hold the plum sites, usually in the centre of the colony – and thus safest from predators – and larger and more securely anchored, while junior birds – the 'newly weds' – have to make do with more vulnerable nests near the edge of the colony. Studies of colonial birds have shown that, not surprisingly, older birds in long-established pairings are more successful, newcomers to breeding less so. Though pairings stable for several seasons are more successful, the 'divorce' of an unsatisfactory pairing and a remating for the next season often leads to a more productive relationship looked at over the several years of the birds' reproductive life.

Arguments against eggs

Most of this discussion has dwelt on the evident successes of egg-laying as a reproductive technique. To set the record straight, it seems sensible to draw attention to those factors operating on the debit side. Eggs are fragile, and thus need protection from breakage – and, of course, the parent birds must exercise constant care when moving about the nest. To develop, eggs need meticulously controlled warmth, maintained over a considerable period. Anyone with experience of incubators (the man-made alternative to the sitting bird), with precise temperature, moisture and egg-rolling control mechanisms, will realize just how essential such accuracy is.

A further factor in eggs' disfavour is that they need additional protection and insulation from adverse extremes of climate – high winds, heavy rainfall, sudden frosts and so on. Moreover, they and the young hatching from them are particularly vulnerable to predators but normally unable to defend themselves, so the construction and concealment of the nest must give a degree of physical protection. As potential predators range from terrestrial snakes and mammals varying in size from field-mice to foxes, through to birds like crows and hawks, and even the Cuckoo, a great deal is being expected of the average nest.

Siting the nest

For the great majority of birds – those with other than a minute territory – within the confines of their territory will be a number of nest sites suitable for that particular species. In multi-brooded species like the Blackbird in the garden or the Stonechat in its gorse patch on the cliff top, such sites may be used, in succession, for different broods. In the case of other birds, like the Wren – usually double-brooded – the male does the bulk of the heavy construction work on several nests, each well-concealed and domed, with a side entrance hole, before the pair together – perhaps with the female playing the leading role – decide on one particular nest. To this they put the finishing touches, largely by adding a soft, warm lining. In a similar way the male Lapwing will form several 'scrapes', scuffing hollows in the ground by using his feet and belly, in suitable areas of field, grassland or moor, before the final site is chosen and a lining of dried grasses added ready to receive the eggs.

In many other birds the female seems to play the major part in deciding where the nest will be, and subsequently in the actual construction of it. In spring the female Blackbird with a beakful of grass like an oversize moustache is a familiar sight, but usually near at hand will be her mate. This pattern is common to many smaller birds: whether the apparently chauvinist role of the male is protective of the female is difficult to say, but clearly she may be pre-occupied and vulnerable, and clearly also he must maintain constant vigilance over the territory as a whole at this competitive time to ensure that its boundaries are maintained against neighbouring birds.

So the biological complexities of the breeding season are already beginning to accumulate: both birds of the pair must get – and maintain – themselves in the peak of condition, which means long hours of feeding. At the same time, however, the territory must be patrolled, defended by song or display, and the nest site selected and the nest built.

Types of nest

What, then, is the range of nest types? It is possible to group them broadly, relating structure to groups of birds and their habitats. But it must be remembered that in birds there are inevitably exceptions to the general rules. One example would be the Woodcock, a member of the wader family, most of which nest on the shore or on open swampy moorland or marshes. The Woodcock, though, breeds deep in the heart of mature woodland, often laying its eggs in a nest lined with dry oak leaves. Another example is the Goldeneye, a duck which nests in holes in trees, and indeed in suitable nestboxes, often high above the ground; most of its relatives nest on the ground close to water.

The simplest of nests are those where the egg or eggs are laid on the ground. Any apparent vulnerability of such a site to predators is often offset by the physical nature of the surroundings: for example, the Guillemot laying on exposed but often inaccessible cliff ledges, additionally protected by the sea. In other cases protection is derived from the concealment provided by the colouring and patterning on the eggs – and subsequently also the young chicks, which have so-called cryptically patterned down.

In many waders – for example, Lapwing, Oystercatcher, Ringed Plover – and game birds – for example, Pheasant and Partridge – this camouflage is staggeringly effective, and the human observer, no matter how certain he may be that he knows where a chick has crouched, must be extremely careful not to tread on it. Camouflage such as this is often only effective when the chick is stationary, so is normally accompanied by well-developed behaviour patterns in which the youngster responds instantly, by crouching, to the warning cries of its parents when a potential predator is approaching. Often it will remain motionless until the predator is literally within centimetres.

Wader nests of this simple type often appear simple scrapes in the ground on superficial inspection, but most do have a structure. They are usually positioned near some feature like a larger rock – often inconspicuous to human eyes – or a tuft of vegetation, and many may actually be ornamented. In one well-documented nest, over 1000 small pebbles, twigs and pieces of shell were arranged around the rim, all identifiably gathered from some distance away.

This simplistic nest pattern is developed further by other waders, by many ducks and gulls, and by most of the larger sea birds like Cormorants and Gannets. Dead vegetation and all manner of flotsam and jetsam – some of it potentially hazardous to the birds, like fragments of fishing nets in which the young may become entangled – is gathered into a mound, with a shallow depression at its centre containing the clutch of eggs. The structure is often bulky but low in cliff-nesting birds and many of the ducks and gulls, but where the nest is built on terrain subject to sudden changes in water levels – as in the case of both coastal- and moorland lake-nesting Black-headed Gulls – it may be built up into a sizeable pyramid. The various swans and the Crane are the most dramatic examples of birds whose nests take this form. The element of height offers extra protection against flooding and the consequent hazards of chilling to the eggs or young.

An actually floating nest is a logical evolutionary development to achieve extra flood protection, and several water birds build in this way, mostly members of the grebe family, but also some marsh terns. A grebe nest is a raft of iris leaves and various water weeds, built well out from the bank but still within the band of peripheral emergent vegetation. The nest is loosely anchored by strands of vegetation to nearby reeds or sedges, and with these 'mooring ropes' it can rise and fall naturally and in tune with either floodwaters or drought.

Great Crested Grebe

Such a nest survives far more satisfactorily than those of Coot or Moorhen in the same freshwater habitats, because their nests are fixed firmly in a clump of reeds or on an overhanging bough and may be either submerged in a flood or left several feet above the mud should water levels fall dramatically. The grebes are specialist water birds, with legs set near the tail of their streamlined bodies, so a flattish, floating nest makes access (and emergency departure) far easier for birds naturally clumsy out of the water.

A further advance in nest design, offering various forms of practical protection, is the cup-shaped nest used by the majority of birds and in particular by the small and medium-sized song birds. The eggs tend to cluster naturally at the base of the cup, and there they, and later the chicks, are safe from physical disturbance by the wind and to some degree concealed from the eyes of predators. The nest is usually built in a suitably strong cluster of twigs or in the fork of a branch, where the outer framework of stout grasses, plant stems and twigs – even branches in the case of larger birds – is firmly lodged. Finer materials are woven on to the inside of this structure, which is often re-inforced with mud, before the nest cup itself is lined with a variety of materials, including dried mud, fine grasses or rootlets, moss, hair, plant down, fur or feathers – all offering excellent thermal insulation for eggs and young.

The basic structural pattern of such nests remains the same even across a wide range of sizes, from a few centimetres diameter in the case of the Chaffinch or Goldfinch to a metre or more for the Golden Eagle and Heron. Sometimes such nests may be further 'decorated' on the outside with plant material gathered from close by. Many Chaffinches' nests – among the neatest of all – have small fragments of lichens woven into the outermost layers, making them masterpieces of camouflage, it being difficult to tell where branch or trunk ends and nest begins.

The domed nest

Domed nests, such as have already been mentioned in the case of the Wren, are further extensions of the cup pattern, the dome – with its side entrance – offering a totally enclosed cavity protecting eggs and young. Wrens' nests are often built in ivy clinging to a trunk, or some other natural crevice, and occasionally in such odd situations as the pocket of an old gardening jacket, hanging temporarily unused in a shed.

Although usually placed deep in a thorny thicket, the Long-tailed Tit's nest is visually more exposed. Made of cobwebs, hair, lichen and moss, the flask-shaped nest of this bird (whose colloquial name is 'bottle tit') has the additional advantage that it is amazingly flexible and can thus accommodate the brood as it grows up! As the young wriggle around, so the walls of the nest can be seen to bulge. Equally amazing is the record of over 2000 feathers, collected by one pair of Long-tailed Tits to line the interior of their nest, each feather necessitating a separate journey by those apparently rather feebly beating wings.

Low-level domed nests are built in undergrowth and rough grass by birds as small as Willow Warblers; high-level and much bulkier ones up in the trees by Magpies. Magpies choose thorny twigs to build their football- (or bigger-) sized nest to give additional protection from other members of the crow family. However, domed nests overall offer better concealment of the eggs or young from a predator's eyes than a simple cup, and thus allow the incubating bird greater opportunity to slip away from the nest for a while to feed or drink.

Altogether different in structure, the House Martin's nest is the same in principle. Ancestrally sited under overhanging cliff ledges, but now 'traditionally' built under the eaves of suitable houses, this bird's nest is built up of small pellets – miniature bricks – of mud gathered from beside puddles, until a quarter-sphere with an orange-segment-shaped entrance slit results. The colour of the mouthful-sized pellets gives a clue to the often distant origin of the nesting material. Sadly, unless the entrance is of precisely small enough dimensions, House Martins' nests all too frequently fall victim to take-overs by that other domestic associate, the House Sparrow.

The protected nest

When nesting, various birds, including several owls, the Stock Dove, Jackdaw and a couple of other tits, seek the protection of natural cavities in old trees, cliff faces and in buildings. Some will use old woodpecker holes, abandoned by their original excavators, and all find nestboxes of various designs perfectly acceptable alternatives to the real thing. Such protection may be more apparent than real, however, as several predators, especially weasels, are well able to climb up to the nests and may become expert at tracking down the squeaking young.

Great Spotted Woodpeckers, recognized as carnivorous on insect larvae, are not normally counted among avian predators, but they are well able to hack their way through – particularly into a nestbox – to reach noisy young, which they devour with relish. Where many nestboxes are in position in a single wood, the local woodpeckers may become so familiar with this process that they recognize nestboxes for what they are and will begin to attack them early in the season to eat the eggs, long before the calls of young birds reveal their contents.

Some Great Spotted Woodpeckers will also exploit a habit of young hole-nesting birds, one which should make the youngster the more successful but which on occasion can be its undoing. Within the nest competition is fierce for food brought by a returning parent, and that parent shows no sign of helping out the poorly fed; it only pushes the food into the nearest, widest-open gape before departing for the next load. Thus the nestlings, eager for a meal and alerted by the shadow of the homecoming parent falling across the entrance hole, jump up to be first in line. Woodpeckers are sometimes alert to this habit, and alight by the hole, immediately reaching in with their beak to grab the expectant, but ultimately unfortunate, youngster and drag it out to eat.

Woodpeckers themselves excavate their own nest holes in standing trees, often in dead but frequently in the living wood. A powerful head and neck, and a strong beak inserted and twisted, tear off flakes of wood in hammer-and-chisel manner. The Willow Tit, too, excavates its own hole, unlike its very close relative, the Marsh Tit. Admittedly, the Willow Tit chooses soft timber, like elder, or partially rotten wood, but by excavating its own nest it does provide a useful identification character to help distinguish it from the very similar Marsh Tit. Most birdwatchers rely on calls to separate the two, so alike are they, but because of its woodpecker-like habit the Willow Tit develops powerful neck muscles that give it an appreciably thicker-necked, bull-headed appearance. This becomes a useful field identification aid to the experienced birdwatcher when, as is often the case, the bird under observation remains stubbornly silent!

Nest burrows

Bee-eaters, Kingfishers and Sand Martins all dig out nest burrows in sandy soils – usually in banks except in the case of the Bee-eater, which often chooses flat land. The initial impact seems to be made with the beak, but once a start has been accomplished the rest of the excavation is carried out with the feet, both male and female usually taking turns in shift work. In an interesting apparent reversal of the processes of evolution and adaptation these three birds – Sand Martin and King-fisher particularly – are characterized by the small size and seemingly ineffectual nature of their feet, especially for such a task, which in avian terms is a most unusual one.

Perhaps less expected as burrow nesters, but certainly better equipped foot-wise for digging, are some of the sea birds. One is the Manx Shear-water whose eerie caterwauling, crowing calls are among the most spec-tacular and spine-chilling of any nocturnal bird song. These cries, coming from cliff tops or from screes high in the hills are suspected of giving rise to Nordic legends of trolls.

Another hole nester is the ever-popular Puffin which, like the Manx Shearwater, is primarily a pelagic bird, coming ashore only to breed. Although both species often use natural crevices in screes or rock falls, and both may oust rabbits from their warrens in the cliff-top turf, Puffins in particular are quite capable of excavating their own burrows with their powerful legs and sharply clawed webbed feet. Again, both sexes take turns in digging.

The world's best-constructed nests

Viewed worldwide, perhaps the most elaborate nest constructions – par-ticularly bearing in mind that one of the 'penalties' that birds have to pay for the ability of flight is the loss of functional hands – are by tropical birds. Probably less well-known are the South American oropendolas which weave flask-shaped nests high in the trees, with a long, pendant, trumpet-shaped entrance tunnel to exclude predators, particularly reptiles. Much the same protection is afforded by the nests of many African sunbirds. Spherical, with a side entrance hole, these are sus-pended from a branch on a slender woven rope of grasses and cobwebs.

The widest variety of such nests, however, is found among the appropriately named weavers, most of which are African birds. Again, the exclusion of predators seems to be the major goal, but it is impossible not to marvel at how such nests are woven – often on swaying slender palm fronds or branch tips – by the use of beak and feet alone.

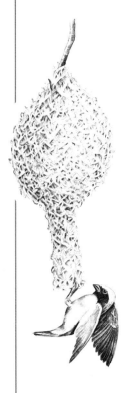

Weaver bird

Nearer to home the accolades for nest construction must go to the Golden Oriole and the minute Goldcrest, both of which suspend hammock-like nests between two appropriately spaced twigs, and to the Reed Warbler. Weaving a basket of grasses around such apparently unsuitable and difficult supports as smooth, vertical reed stems is one thing, but that this structure should be capable of withstanding gales and, not infrequently, the unwanted and disproportionately huge weight of a full-grown young Cuckoo is tribute indeed.

Bird with no nest: the Cuckoo

Though there are several families in the world adopting the same tactics, the Cuckoo is notorious as a nest parasite. The Cuckoo makes no nest at all but lays in a foster nest and then leaves the foster parents to raise its young – so there are no problems of incubation or brooding for the Cuckoo itself. Perhaps this parasitism should be regarded as one example, at least, of the ultimate in sophisticated breeding strategies.

Gearing family size to food supply

In the long course of evolution, several patterns of egg laying have emerged among the various families of birds. Much as with the egg *versus* foetus debate, there is no clearly defined better or worse approach: each has evolved to be effective in particular circumstances. These circumstances may change the pattern even within a species. For example, in Britain the majority of Blue and Great Tits depend on the caterpillars of the winter moth, which occur predominantly on oak and other broad-leaved trees, to feed their young. These caterpillars usually occur in enormous numbers, but only for less than a month in early summer when the oak leaves are young, pale yellow-green and succulent, lacking the tannins that will protect them from caterpillar attack later in the year. To match this short, sharp peak of food abundance in Britain, the vast majority of Blue and Great Tits are single-brooded, laying just one clutch of eggs – though this may be replaced if lost to predators.

By marvellous but not yet fully understood means, the tits time laying and hatching to a nicety in most years, and often seem able to gear the size of the clutch to suit the level of abundance of their caterpillar food source. In this way, the nestful of youngsters is at its most demanding at the same time as the caterpillars reach full size, thus making the feeding of them much more efficient.

On the Continent, many Blue and Great Tits inhabit coniferous woodland. Here, though caterpillars are readily available, they are never so abundant as the winter moth is on oak. The caterpillar 'season' is, however, very much longer, extending well into summer. These conifer-dwelling tits are normally double-brooded, but each brood is relatively small for the species at around eight eggs, so effectively both British and Continental birds are attempting to raise the same number of young but over differing time scales.

In further contrast to the almost literally 'all eggs in one basket' approach of British Blue and Great Tits are the majority of small and medium-sized song birds. A great many of these – several familiar as garden birds, like the Blackbird and Song Thrush, so easily observed near the house – usually produce two or three clutches (sometimes more in a good summer), each of four to six eggs. This allows them to exploit food supplies which occur at varying but moderate levels throughout the summer, rather than in a single, short-lived glut. In all such cases it seems that the available appropriate food supply, in each type of ecological niche, is exploited to maximum effect.

Food supply as a method of population control

Larger birds, of course, may not have the time or available food supplies to form more than one or two eggs, or alternatively to raise their young successfully through a long period of dependence. In these cases it seems overall that food is the dominant factor in determining clutch size. Perhaps the best examples of this are to be found among the owls, and none better than the Short-eared Owl, like many of its relatives heavily dependent on small rodents as a food source but, unlike them, primarily a daytime hunter.

Short-eared Owls nest on open rough land, moors and marshes, laying in a shallow scrape among the low vegetation. Voles form the major part of their food, and it is well established that the numbers of these rodents fluctuate considerably. The normal pattern of events is that after usually four years of steady increase, the vole population peaks and then crashes as the available food is incapable of supporting it. From these rock-bottom levels, numbers begin again to increase. When vole numbers are really low, the Short-eared Owls may lay just one or two eggs, and some pairs may not lay at all, leaving areas of suitable – and normally occupied – terrain quite devoid of owls for a year or two. If voles are really abundant, the clutch size may reach double figures and most of the emerging chicks will fledge: a most effective birth-rate control mechanism.

Food supply can also strongly influence the timing of the breeding season, as in the cases of the Blue and Great Tits already mentioned. Another good example of this phenomenon occurs in the Crossbill, which because of its highly specialized feeding technique (see Chapter 4) is largely dependent on the seeds lying hidden deep within the segments of conifer cones. Strangely, these cones may mature at various times of the year, including the winter months. In consequence, as they attempt to exploit localized food abundance for breeding purposes, it is possible to find Crossbills sitting on eggs as autumn turns into winter, sometimes incubating with snow on their backs.

In much the same way Ravens, depending for food largely on the placentas at the late-winter birth of hill-farming lambs, and on the carrion derived from the casualties inevitable after lambing in such severe weather, now start breeding even in February, despite the climate at that time up in the hills.

Incubating the eggs

The incubation period – the time taken for the fertilized embryo to develop into a chick and then break out of the eggshell – varies considerably. As a general rule, larger species tend to have longer incubation periods than smaller ones, but this rule is by no means inviolate. Most song birds start incubating their eggs only when the clutch is complete and sit pretty consistently for around a fortnight – sometimes a day or so more or less. As an elegant further adaptation to the Cuckoo's already sophisticated mode of parasitism, this bird's eggs often hatch in only eleven or twelve days, so giving the young Cuckoo the chance to shoulder its foster parents' own eggs out of the nest before they hatch: an easier, less energy-costly exercise than evicting struggling nestlings.

Ascending the size scale, pigeons' and woodpeckers' eggs take a few days longer than those of the song birds, but normally less than three weeks. Three weeks is a fair average, too, for many waders, gulls and smaller ducks, but interestingly is also about the time that the eggs of the Swift – a comparatively small bird – take to hatch. Owls, larger ducks and geese incubate for about a month, while the pen Mute Swan sits for around thirty-five days. At the top of the list for Western Europe, longest of all incubation periods are those of the Golden Eagle and the Gannet, each sitting for about forty-five days.

The females of many species – and occasionally also the males of some smaller birds where both sexes share the incubation – develop a 'brood patch' at the start of the breeding season when some of the breast and belly down feathers are *shed* (contrary to popular expectation) to expose an oval patch of skin, wrinkled and dark reddish or purple in colour because it is so rich in superficial blood vessels. Through this wrinkled skin and its blood supply, body heat is transferred (hot-water-bottle-like) from the incubating bird to its eggs. When a bird settles down with cautious shuffles on to her (or his) eggs to begin brooding, these movements ensure that all the eggs are positioned beneath, and in contact with, the brood patch. Before it settles down, the sitting bird erects the remaining breast and belly feathers and, as it sits, these enclose the eggs, serving as an insulating coverlet.

In the case of some sea birds, like the Gannet, the brood patch is absent. This could be a relatively primitive feature, or it might be that the possession of a brood patch could lead to an overly large loss of body heat for a bird spending much of its time with its belly in contact with cold waters. In the case of the Gannet, and its tropical relatives the boobies, the use of the feet compensates for the lack of a brood patch. These are large, and all four toes are joined by webbing which is carefully folded over the egg beneath the sitting bird, allowing the veins in the feet to pass the warmth of the blood to the egg.

Penguins face even greater hazards: not only are temperatures low in general in their Antarctic habitat, but often they will also be breeding on ice or frozen ground. The larger species (King and Emperor) incubate in a vertical position, and solve the problem of temperature by resting their single large egg across their feet, thus insulating it from the icy ground beneath, and enveloping it in a tea-cosy-like muffler of skin rich in blood vessels and with a thick layer of sub-cutaneous blubber.

Often the female will do all, or almost all, of the incubation, leaving the nest only briefly a few times a day to feed and drink. This is particularly the case among the song birds where the male rarely does much of the incubating, though he may more frequently brood the small

*Male Red-necked
Phalarope
brooding young*

young. This unequal split of 'duty' is one reason why, in so many birds, the plumage of the female is superficially drab: it provides excellent camouflage for her – and the nest – during the hazardous period of incubation. In contrast, it can be argued that the male needs his more colourful plumage both to attract a mate and to defend his territory to best effect. Among the larger non-passerine birds, incubation is quite commonly a shared involvement between the sexes in the divers, grebes, waders, gulls, terns, skuas, auks and pigeons; even among the smaller near-passerines like the woodpeckers and the Swift and Kingfisher, male and female take turns at incubating.

Role reversal: the Red-necked Phalarope

Only very exceptionally, as in the case of the Red-necked Phalarope, will the male assume total responsibility for hatching the eggs and raising the young. Interestingly, in the case of the Phalarope the domestic roles of male and female are to a degree reversed, and it is she who (in contrast to most other species) is the more brightly coloured and who takes the lead in display. She is also slightly larger than her mate.

Though some breed as far south as Scotland and Ireland, most Red-necked Phalaropes are summer visitors to Arctic or near-Arctic tundra, breeding beside small, shallow lakes. For them, as for several other ducks, geese and waders, time is at a premium if they are to breed successfully during the short, climatically unpredictable Arctic summer. Though food, in the form mostly of insects and their larvae, may be hugely abundant, it is only so for a few brief weeks.

By evolving the reversal of sexual roles, the Red-necked Phalarope has arrived at a novel way of increasing its productivity. Arriving on

Red-necked Phalaropes feeding, female in foreground

the breeding grounds, the female displays and solicits a mate. Once he has fertilized her, she lays her clutch of eggs in a well-concealed nest and then leaves the male with total responsibility for their upbringing. Having established one mate on a nest, she moves away to find and court another and, after a second mating, leaves him too incubating a brood. It is clear that the male's greater need for camouflage is the reason for his dowdier plumage. By avoiding many of the safety hazards and strength-sapping processes that a hen bird normally has to survive, the female Red-necked Phalarope directs the bulk of her energies towards maximizing egg production in a way that allows a good chance of raising two broods of young in a time span only slightly greater than that taken by most waders to raise a single brood.

Breeding seasons not governed by time

Having looked at Arctic (and Antarctic) and temperate climates, it is only proper to consider also the influence of the tropics on breeding seasons. Rather as for many waders it is the state of the tide, not the time of night or day, that governs feeding activity, so for many tropical birds it is the coming of the rainy season (or seasons) that dictate the pattern of breeding. During the rains, and in the weeks after they have finished, plant growth is lush and insect life abundant. Soon after, fruit and seeds are plentiful, but by the time the dry season is a couple of months old, an increasingly arid landscape begins to offer less and less to breeding birds.

Naturalists from temperate or cold regions of the globe tend also to think in terms of a marked seasonality in bird occurrence, and certainly in bird breeding seasons. For tropical sea birds, however, especially those breeding on oceanic islands, other factors may dictate the speed at which the 'clock' that governs their lives functions. Food and nest sites may be available year-round for many sea birds like some of the terns and albatrosses. It seems that instead of an annual, seasonally governed, twelve-month year, the 'year' for such sea birds is dictated by the time it takes them to complete one breeding cycle and get back into condition for the next. For smaller sea birds like the terns and noddies, this cycle may be as short as nine months, while for larger ones, like the albatrosses with their fledgling in the nest for several months, eighteen months may pass before they are capable of breeding again.

The hatching period

Most smaller birds' clutches of eggs hatch entirely within about twenty-four hours, but in those larger birds where eggs are laid at two-day (or longer) intervals, and where incubation starts as soon as the first egg is laid, the eggs will hatch at similar intervals. This gives rise to a considerable size discrepancy in the young, noticeable in birds like the Golden Eagle. Normally this results in the execution of the smaller chick by the larger, to the despair of conservationists anxious to see an increase in numbers of birds of this degree of rarity.

Size discrepancy is also very evident in broods of young owls: in years when voles are plentiful and clutches of eggs large, there may be a two-week difference in age, and size, between the oldest and the youngest chick. This offers the owls an unusual facility for a further measure of effective birth control, for should the available food supply falter or diminish for any reason, the oldest chick will eat the smallest and then the next smallest to eke out the shortened rations that the parent birds are able to supply. Although obviously distressful and distasteful to human eyes, this is actually a very effective way of ensuring that at least one or two youngsters fledge successfully, rather than the whole brood, all fed equally poorly, perishing from starvation.

The young birds emerge from the egg slowly, using a small, calcareous 'egg tooth' (like a miniaturized rhinoceros horn) on the tip of the beak to cut through the egg membranes and fracture the shell. For some time before hatching – up to a few days, depending on the length of the incubation period – the unhatched chick will have been in communication with its parent by means of piping calls from within the egg, but parental help during this slow emergence is often limited to the removal of the shell from which the chick has hatched. The egg tooth is lost soon after hatching.

In the case of most smaller birds – particularly those grouped together as song and perching birds in the order Passeriformes – the youngsters that hatch from the egg are naked, blind and quite helpless. They remain in this rather ugly, reptilian state for several days, totally dependent on their parents, and the actual nest structure, for food and warmth and, just as important, for protection from both adverse climatic conditions and from predators. Hence the parents of such nestlings – technically called 'nidicolous' young – have an energy-sapping programme, collecting adequate food to provide for ever-hungry mouths and yet spending much time in attendance at the nest brooding the young to supply warmth and shelter.

The nestlings develop into fledglings within the confines of the nest – a process usually taking two or three weeks for smaller birds, depending on their size but also, to a considerable degree, on the weather both during their nestling period and at the time they are due to fledge, or leave the nest. At this stage bad weather will often confine them to the nest for the extra day or two. The young of larger birds take much longer to fledge – the Golden Eagle two months or more and the Gannet over three months.

Leaving the nest

The majority of song birds actually remain within the nest until a few hours before they leave it for good, because to fall to the ground during a period of wing exercising could increase the risk of discovery by a predator such as a weasel or lead to the chick's abandonment by its parents. The chicks of most gulls, however, may leave the nest cup – soon trodden down into a platform – and shelter under nearby vegetation, emerging only to be fed.

Yet for the Kittiwake, which builds a precarious nest glued with guano, saliva and mud to the smallest of rock projections on a cliff face – often under an overhang – small-bird rules must apply, because if the nestling strays from the nest confines before it can fly, it will almost certainly plunge to its death. The same goes for the young Heron in its nest high in the trees. Although it is capable of clambering about gawkily among the branches, should it fall a short distance, still remaining close to the nest but unable to get back up to it, it too will perish, as its parents' rigid behaviour patterns allow them to feed by regurgitation only on the nest cup, and they will take no notice of any chicks outside the nest, no matter how noisily they are calling for food.

Young Swallows, however, may return to the nest to roost overnight for some days, or even weeks, after they have fledged, especially when the weather is poor. As their parents may use the nest for a subsequent brood, and seem to take no exception to the return of the young, this can lead to as many as ten or a dozen nestlings, fledglings and their parents on the nest at once.

For the young of many of the larger birds, things are very different. Ducks, gulls and waders are the best conforming examples among this group, while the birds of prey and many sea birds like Cormorants and Auks are striking exceptions to the norm. Taking the Redshank, a typical estuary wader, as an example, the chick hatches already covered in down and within a few hours is dry and able to leave the nest. Its eyes are open from birth and it has well-developed legs that allow it to run actively almost immediately, and to swim if necessary to escape danger. Its downy feathers provide warmth, so that brooding by a parent is chiefly a night-time necessity, and in addition are so patterned as to provide a most effective camouflage. If danger threatens, the parents shriek a warning and the youngster crouches, quite motionless, until the potential predator has departed.

These nidifugous young (literally 'fleeing the nest') are able to scamper about and feed themselves at only a few hours old, and usually range far from the nest. In the case of waders, often the family – normally four or less – is split between the two parents as they move about and feed. In the case of the ducks, the male may be far away and certainly takes no part in the rearing of the ducklings, who often remain under the alert guardianship of their mother. In some species, like the Shelduck and the Eider, large crèches of ducklings may gather together under the protection of two or three adults, though how these supervisory tasks are apportioned remains an intriguing mystery.

Once nidifugous young leave the nest, they continue to need parental care and training in feeding techniques, usually for a maximum of several days in the case of smaller birds, but for many weeks in the case of the Tawny Owl. Young Tawny Owls establish regular feeding posts where they wait, calling with anxious 'ku-witts' for parental attention. It is not until late summer or early autumn, when the parents need to re-establish territories, that this care and attention ceases, to be replaced by increasingly vigorous antagonism as the young attempt to resist being driven away.

Helping out with younger siblings

In some nidifugous species like the Moorhen, the fledged young of the first brood may stay on the home pond or stream and help to feed their brothers and sisters from later broods. Assistance with breeding activities may also be more widespread than previously suspected among smaller birds. Called co-operative breeding, most recorded instances involve 'helpers at the nest', but recent reports include pre-nesting 'help' with unlikely operations such as mate attraction and courtship. Such behaviour is rather more commonplace among tropical and sub-tropical birds like the Bee-eaters, Manakins and Babblers, but there are increasing records of breeding-season assistance in temperate birds, including the homely but enigmatic Dunnock and the Long-tailed Tit. This is an area of bird biology which is of great fascination, and one where a considerable increase in both recorded instances and in our understanding of them is to be expected over the next few years.

A period of vulnerability

Even among those birds that are too often easily dismissed as 'ordinary', the nestling stage is a time of very considerable risk. Nidifugous young must rely on their camouflage plumage and speedy – and continued – reaction to warning cries from parents that must ever be on the alert while trying to guard active, food-seeking offspring running in several directions at the same time. Nidicolous young are in a way captives of their nest, and may be noisy and inexperienced, easily drawing the attention of a predator to themselves. As their parents have to spend almost all of the daylight hours in ceaseless attempts to keep them well fed, after the first couple of days – when their food demands are least – they are brooded, to keep them warm, less and less often by the female who has increasingly also to hunt for food.

In the early days of young finches, however, even this may not be the routine that could easily be supposed. Though the finches are basically seed eaters, many species feed small, protein-rich insects to their young for the first few days, an operation that necessitates a complete change to alien feeding techniques. As they are brooded less, so in consequence they become more vulnerable to predators, to cold and particularly to heavy rain or hailstorms.

How the Swift copes with hard times

In the Swift, a specialist insect feeder and among the most totally aerial of birds, and in consequence particularly prone to food shortages during the spells of bad weather that characterize the west and north of its summer range in Europe, the young have evolved a technique to improve survival over lean times. Unlike most small nestlings, which quickly chill and die, even naked young Swifts can reduce their body metabolism: heartbeat and respiration rates drop and their body temperature slowly falls. The chicks enter a torpor – in effect a short-term hibernation (or rather aestivation). The parent birds cannot, of course, remain to brood them for warmth, as they must depart in front of, or around, the weather system in search of better feeding.

It seems likely from radar observations of Swift colonies that, in Western Europe, such journeys away from adverse weather in search of food may last several days and cover several hundred kilometres of non-stop flight. As the weather in the nesting area improves, and insect food again becomes available, so (like reptiles) the youngsters warm up and begin to resume normal life and growth again, and the parent birds return and recommence feeding.

In a typical Atlantic seaboard summer, with alternating fine spells and periods of wet weather, the feather growth of the young Swift reflects the vagaries of the climate. When the weather is poor and food intake low, the actual feather proteins are laid down less robustly than when the weather and feeding are good. Holding such a feather up to the light in autumn reveals a banded appearance, similar to the annual growth rings in trees. This allows a remarkably accurate assessment to be made of the good times, and bad, and their severity and duration, during the summer just past!

The astonishing breeding habits of the Emperor Penguin

How much more severe, though, are the climatic rigours that young Emperor Penguins must endure in the remote fastnesses of their Antarctic breeding grounds. Few birds can lead such cold lives, and only rarely will an Emperor Penguin set foot on actual land, as its time is divided between the food-rich but icy waters just off the Antarctic ice shelf and the breeding colony, normally situated on the ice cap itself.

Quite astonishingly, though evidently also successfully, the Emperors seem to throw down the gauntlet to the weather by returning ashore in March, during the Antarctic autumn. They waddle across the ice fields, often for many kilometres, to ancestral breeding grounds where they display and pair up. In May, at the start of the ferocious winter and at a time when there is virtually no daylight, the female lays her single egg and almost immediately transfers it to the feet and brood pouch of her mate. He will then stand, back to the icy winds and snow-storms, incubating for just over sixty days. Winds may reach 160kph (100mph), and temperatures may drop to $-40°C$ ($-40°F$): to alleviate the cold the males group together in 'pods', and seem to take turns in forming the outermost protective ring of bodies and enjoying the comparative warmth of the centre of the huddle.

During this period the briefest exposure of the egg to the climate would be fatal to the embryo. The male parent, of course, cannot feed and must survive on fat stored around his body during the food-plentiful long days of summer. The female, meanwhile, has walked back to the sea and is busy feeding, to return, enormously plump, to the colony within a couple of days of the hatching of the chick. She then takes over the parental duties of keeping the newborn infant warm and well fed, while the male in his turn journeys to the sea to replenish his depleted bodily reserves before also returning, laden with food, to help raise the growing youngster, a task shared for about four months.

This is no easy time to grow up, but larger young are well protected by dense down and a thick layer of subcutaneous blubber, and they too gather in larger huddles to ward off the severest storms. The breeding season lasts about six months – all of them winter ones, which seems difficult to explain: perhaps matters are arranged this way so that the chick's independence coincides with the start of the Antarctic spring, allowing it to begin its life at sea at a time when food is becoming most plentiful.

Co-operation of the sexes in raising young: the Sparrowhawk

When it comes to raising young, among birds the division of the labours of feeding between the sexes varies widely between species. Most drakes pay little or no attention to their family responsibilities from as early as the laying of the clutch, leaving all the hard work to the duck, but in the majority of birds the labours are shared roughly equally, as in the case of species as diverse in habits and habitat as the Blackbird and the Lapwing. In some instances the balance is much more subtle and actually changes as the nestlings grow older: the Sparrowhawk provides one of the better examples.

In most birds of prey, the female is much larger than the male, and in the Sparrowhawk this is particularly striking, as she may weigh over 250 grams, he less than 150. As a natural consequence of this size and weight difference, the male takes on average much smaller prey, concentrating on woodland birds like tits and finches, while the female, though not scorning smaller birds on occasions, tends to feed on thrush-sized birds and can tackle prey up to the size of a Woodpigeon.

The female carries the brunt of incubation, and because (contrary perhaps to popular belief) the nests of birds of prey are just as vulnerable to predators as others, she must also guard the nest closely in the first days after hatching. In fact, Goshawks greatly favour eating the nestlings of their smaller relative, the Sparrowhawks. At this early stage, the lightweight male can cope with the food demands of the brood but, as they grow, he becomes less able to do so.

Hunting Sparrowhawk

At this time the female takes over the role of major food provider – something she can carry out more effectively because of her greater killing power. As a further subtle embellishment to this evolutionary strategy, though most birds moult old and worn feathers after the breeding season is over, the female Sparrowhawk moults while incubating and brooding the small young, so when she does resume hunting it is on wings freshly moulted and at peak performance.

Survival of the fittest

Often the larger broods of many birds may contain one or two weak-lings, called 'runts', which will normally survive only in years when food is really abundant. Parent birds returning to the nest do not follow human sympathetic behaviour patterns and succour the weak: they are under great pressure from hungry young to supply sufficient food and usually push their beakful into the widest-open gape emerging furthest and most prominently from the huddle of young in the nest. Though the runt may be equally or even more hungry, it is too weak to compete effectively in this struggle, so it is usually one of the strongest chicks that gets fed and no attempt is made to give extra support to weaklings. Only when the others are satisfied and dozing while digesting their meal will the runt stand any chance. In this way it is the fittest of the youngsters that survive, rather than the whole brood being placed at risk of being weakened and ultimately lost in order to try to save the runts.

In most harassed parent birds, the upturned yellow-rimmed gape of the nestling, coupled with its hunger squeaks, produces a sufficient stimulus to feed the young. Many young song birds also have a recogniz-able pattern of spots within the mouth which helps to prevent any con-fusion with nearby nests of other species – these are readily visible in Dunnocks. Such palate markings can operate as a coding, or a sort of password, that constitutes an additional hazard to any would-be nest parasite. This ruse has been successfully overcome, however, by the Whydahs of Africa, small seed-eating birds laying their eggs in the nests of other finch species: young Whydah closely mimics the pattern of mouth spots of its foster siblings.

The young Cuckoo, with its particularly wheedling cry and rich orange-crimson gape, also seems able to overcome these identification barriers. Once it has left its foster nest, and is ensconced in a bush or on top of a post nearby, it seems able to stop almost any food-carrying bird in its tracks and draw it, remorselessly, to deposit the food load in the Cuckoo's gaping maw, no matter how unlike their own young it appears. At least one unfortunate Wren, perching on a young Cuckoo's head and leaning over to push some food into its mouth, is on record as actually losing its footing and falling into the capacious throat, in the process suffocating both itself and the Cuckoo.

The key to a meal

In some other birds extraordinarily sophisticated ritual feeding patterns have developed, and these must be gone through before the chick is allowed to eat. The Heron's feeding behaviour has already been mentioned, but probably the most easily observed of such rituals, and one of the best researched, is the Herring Gull's. No matter how plaintive the hunger calls of the young gull, nor how submissive its posture – or, indeed, when it is older, how raucously it *demands* to be fed – it is imperative that the chick pecks at the red spot, conspicuous near the tip of the yellow lower mandible of the parent's beak. This pecking action, coupled with a head-held-low submissive stance, elicits the feeding response in the adult, and from its bulging crop it will disgorge a meal (ranging from fish to waste gleaned from refuse tips) which is quickly bolted down by the young.

Avian reproduction: a successful system?

To human eyes, most birds apparently go to a great deal of trouble through the spring and summer months, and to lay a remarkably large number of eggs. The question then arises as to how effective the avian reproductive system is in maintaining population levels, and two case histories, deliberately involving very different birds, must quickly dispel any doubts on the matter. The Fulmar, a sea bird in size and plumage reminiscent of a gull, but actually a member of a family considered to be relatively primitive, the tube-noses or petrels, is the first.

Fulmars generally choose to nest on remote coastal cliffs. They may take eight years to reach maturity and actual breeding condition, but will have visited the colonies and probably established some form of territory and perhaps a pair bond for a couple of summers previously. Once mature, they lay but a single egg annually, and seem not to replace that egg should it be lost to a predator or as a result of bad weather. This seems a precarious state of affairs, and it is only recently, when detailed results of long-term studies of ringed birds have become available, that our understanding of it is growing.

One major problem was that the Fulmars were outliving the numbered metal rings placed on their legs for identification purposes, but stronger metals and colour-coded plastics removed this obstacle to reveal that many of the species may live for thirty years or more, placing them among the longest-lived of birds. To maintain population levels the pair need only to replace themselves by rearing two chicks to adulthood during their lifetime, which even at the rate of a single egg each year seems readily achievable if the breeding life span is in excess of twenty years. When food supplies are good, as they seem to have been over the last century, this maintenance level may be easily exceeded. Hence the dramatic spread of the Fulmar right around the coasts of Britain. This expansion started from its single stronghold on the cliffs of the remote St Kilda group, off the Outer Hebrides, back in 1872. Besides cliffs Fulmars now nest in sand dunes, quarries some distance inland, and on ledges on large coastal buildings.

Fulmar

The second case concerns a far more familiar bird, the Blue Tit, where the approach is markedly different. As has already been mentioned, the Blue Tit in Britain is normally single-brooded, and thus perhaps slightly atypical of small birds in general. If, however, its single-brood approach is considered to be, if anything, rather more risk-prone than the two, three or four broods of, say, the Blackbird, the arithmetic that follows errs on the right side.

For simplicity's sake, suppose on average that each pair may raise ten young. Studies of ringed birds – always of great value – tell us that adult mortality from year to year is about fifty per cent, which means that on average a pair is made up of one experienced adult and one yearling bird breeding for the first time. Thus, of the ten young around in midsummer, only one need survive through until the next breeding season if population numbers are to be maintained. If Blue Tit numbers are not to escalate violently, this implies something of the order of ninety per cent juvenile mortality – a staggering figure in human terms. Grossly simplifying, we know from ringing results that losses to weasels and Sparrowhawks can each reach a seemingly high thirty per cent, but even this still leaves a slack of thirty per cent to allow scope for other hazards.

Summing up, the avian reproductive system is far from uniform in pattern and immensely varied when it comes to finer details. In essence, it is a whole gallery of masterpieces of effective adaptation to needs and to possibilities. It could be described as conservative in its tendency to overproduction to allow for subsequent hazard, but it certainly allows enough flexibility to tide birds over most troubles and to maintain population levels in all but the most extraordinary circumstances. Even then – for example, after winters of extreme severity – rapid recovery seems normally to be possible. Clearly, if further evidence is required, the abundance and variety of birds in all habitats should be taken as clear proof of the success of their reproductive strategies.

6 Diversity

It is difficult to find a region, almost anywhere on this earth, that is without birds. They may be present only in certain seasons of the year, but otherwise from mid-ocean to mountaintop, from densest jungle to most arid desert, there are birds. Perhaps one of the greatest fascinations of birdwatching as a hobby, or of ornithology as a study (for those with a deepening interest), is the sheer diversity of birds and their structural and behavioural adaptations to the various ways of life that enable them to abound in such variety around us.

The preceding chapters in this book have examined in some detail the ancestry and evolution of birds, their peculiarities, specialities and anatomical adaptations; the myriad ways that they have developed to keep themselves well fed and to maintain their numbers by effective nest-building and reproductive strategies. Possible examples are legion, but the two following encapsulate the ways in which birds' successes have been achieved.

Blue Tit

Few of us, unless we live far to the north or on offshore islands, are likely to escape seeing Blue Tits. Popular because they are widespread and common, they capture the interest all the more because of their habit of frequenting garden bird tables and their readiness to breed in nestboxes put up for them by man. Blue Tits are most agile as feeders and must be among the most nimble of birds. They have little problem hanging upside down on swinging fat, a bag of peanuts or piece of coconut in the garden, a reflection of their natural acrobatic habits when feeding at the extreme tips of woodland branches. They do a great pest-control job for the gardener by eating aphids, caterpillars and other insect pests, but they have earned some notoriety, too, in both rural and urban areas for their attacks on milk bottles. Despite their high mortality rate (see Chapter 5), Blue Tits remain abundant: perhaps it is almost more puzzling to wonder why they do not sometimes become super-abundant?

Success in numbers

If sheer increase in numbers is an indication of success, Herring Gulls – currently expanding their population at a phenomenal ten per cent per annum – deserve the title of the most successful birds of the twentieth century. The majority breed on rocky coasts where the cliffs are sufficiently towering to be undisturbed by man. In north and west, in the absence of man, they will breed on low rocky islets and sand dunes. As numbers increase, huge and dense gulleries are forming. This expansion is putting considerable pressure on other coastal birds, a problem which is discussed earlier in this book.

There are now a number of inland colonies of Herring Gulls in remote moorland areas, and many instances of them breeding on rooftops in coastal towns. This habit started in Dover in the 1920s and has spread rapidly. The raucous 'dawn chorus' of Herring Gulls, which starts in the early hours of the morning, and liberal aerial bombardment of unsuspecting holidaymakers with droppings has led to a sharp fall in the popularity of the 'seagull'.

It is strange to think that, at the turn of the century, gulls were rare birds inland. Today it would be difficult to spend a day anywhere in Britain without seeing numbers of several gull species, and the sight of straggling 'V' formations heading for the coast or nearby lake or reservoir is commonplace towards dark. What is the reason for this change? Probably that gulls exhibit great versatility in feeding, which has led to changes in distribution. The smaller gulls – Common and Black-headed – exploit the opportunities offered by farming: following the plough and eating worms is a good example. But, as we have seen, all the gulls exploit refuse – the visible and, to them, edible evidence of man's increasing affluence and living standards during the century.

The crop-damage controversy

Many of our smaller birds, and indeed some of the larger ones too, are well suited in their numbers, powers of recruitment, mobility and generally catholic diets to damage agricultural crops. Bullfinch depradation was discussed in Chapter 4, and even the homely Blue Tit can cause severe damage to ripening pears: it is this bird – not the wasps usually blamed – that is responsible for the small blemishes and cavities on the shoulder of the fruit, often subsequently invaded by destructive brown rot.

Fortunately, the full damage potential of birds is rarely realized, and crops normally feature only sporadically in the diets of avian pests, which largely depend for much or even all of the year on wild plants. Unlike in most other groups of animals, including insects, there are no 'specialist pests' among the birds dependent for all or much of the year on man's crops. One consequence of this lack is that the occurrence, and the level, of bird damage is influenced by several more or less natural factors, which include changes in climate but among which the availability of natural foods probably predominates.

Some 'unnatural' factors may also play a major role, particularly those related to the location and management of the crop and its surroundings. Attempting to establish a pear orchard adjacent to woodland with well-developed undergrowth is laying it wide open to Bullfinch damage. Similarly, draining coastal marshland to convert it from rough grazing to cereal or arable production is asking for attack by various kinds of winter-visiting geese anxious for a good meal easily obtained. Giving thought to such ecological factors before introducing new cropping systems must often be far more cost-effective in avoiding or minimizing crop damage by birds than the use of gas-fired bangers, scarecrows or other deterrent devices ever can be.

Wide-ranging performance and longevity

It is in their sheer physique that the most eye-arresting examples of birds' adaptations to their lives may be found. To borrow analogies from the world of the motor car, though there are a great many routine production models, there is also a comprehensive range of custom-built sports and even some racing models in which the avian anatomy is particularly well adapted to a specialist life style. The power for these is derived from advanced design of heart, circulatory system, lungs (and air sacs) and digestive system which combine to produce the equivalent of a high-performance (or 'GT') model.

High performance is not necessarily at the cost of a shorter life span, though. 'Average' lives of birds are difficult to calculate in a way meaningful in human terms because they are so biased by the very high levels of mortality in the first few months. Given that they survive these hazardous times, the range of longevity recorded in birds is impressive for creatures of their size lacking the various aids – especially medicinal ones – that we use to prolong our lives.

Recoveries of ringed or colour-marked birds tell us a great deal beyond details of their migratory routes and timings. From such recoveries we can draw generalities on how length of life is related to body weight, though there are exceptions: for example, terns tend to live longer than their weight would suggest.

The smallest and lightest of the world's birds is the Bee Hummingbird, which weighs almost the same as a pygmy shrew at about 2 grams. At the other end of the scale, the Ostrich weighs in at about 135 kilograms, and the 'competition' for the title of heaviest *flying* bird is between the Wandering Albatross – top of the wingspan list at 3.5 metres – and the Dalmatian Pelican, Wild Turkey, Trumpeter Swan and Great Bustard, with individuals of each species reaching the 13 kilogram mark.

It is also possible to calculate some life-expectation figures, once birds have reached adulthood. To generalize again: having survived the high mortality rates of the first year, the 'average' small passerine has a further life expectation of just under one year, while a Woodpigeon could expect about two more years, and a Swift four and a half. At the top end of the scale worldwide is the Royal Albatross, breeding on islands south-east of New Zealand, which can expect almost thirty-three more years once it has become adult.

Age records

Absolute length-of-life records may not mean too much in biological terms, but they are fascinating. In the wild, again it is ring recoveries and detailed long-term studies of colour-marked birds that provide our information. Currently, the record is held by a thirty-six-year-old Oystercatcher, with a Royal Albatross and an Arctic Tern close behind. In the twenty-year-plus bracket fall such birds as Mallard, Mute Swan,

Manx Shearwater, Long-eared Owl, White Stork and, amazingly, Swift! Though a large bird, the oldest Capercaillie that we know of was just under ten – perhaps a reflection of the hazards of life as a game bird!

Among the generally much smaller passerine birds, two species make the record charts in the twenty-plus bracket: Blackbird and Starling, with Rook only just behind. The oldest recorded Bullfinch was over seventeen, the oldest Swallow sixteen – think of its lifetime mileage! Robin and House Sparrow have both topped twelve, but most lie below ten years of age, typical examples being the Dunnock at nine and Dipper at eight. The oldest known Goldcrest and Treecreeper are around seven.

In captivity, of course, life is much safer and most captive birds should live considerably longer than their wild cousins. At the moment probably the oldest bird known (with reliable records to prove it) is a Sulphur-crested Cockatoo in the London Zoo. This came into the collection in 1925 but had been with its previous owner since about 1902, so with certainty it can be said to be over eighty!

With increasingly durable rings (especially on long-lived sea birds) and with the passing of time in long-term studies, it is to be expected that most or all of these record ages will be surpassed in the future. More important, much more light will be thrown on how population dynamics work, and on how recruitment (the addition of successful fledglings to the population) and mortality adjust to match fluctuations in total population numbers.

The speed of flight

Flight speeds, too – bearing in mind the sizes of birds – reflect their high-performance physiology; indeed, they may be one cause of it. Though it may seem simple to measure the speed of a flying bird while driving a motor car, getting really accurate results in known weather conditions – particularly discovering the speed of any head or tail wind at the time – is extremely difficult and has been achieved in the case of relatively few species. Soon after the advent of the motor car, observers were 'clocking' small hedgerow birds at speeds in the region of 30 to 40kph ($18\frac{1}{2}$–25mph), which from modern records seems about right for tits, finches, thrushes and the like.

Generally, despite appearances to the contrary, it seems that the larger birds fly faster: the maximum recorded speed for a Swift is 40kph (25mph), while Woodpigeons have been timed at 61kph (38mph). Other birds with accurately measured speeds in excess of 60kph ($37\frac{1}{4}$mph) include Red-throated Diver, Barnacle Goose, Mallard,

Crane and, fastest on record, the Eider Duck at 76kph (47¼mph). Several of these would be far from the birdwater's obvious choice of a high-speed bird, while such apparently fast-movers as Dunlin, Sparrowhawk and Kestrel are on record as flying at only between 40 and 50kph (25 and 31mph)!

Much of the spectrum of avian behaviour and physique is summed up in one of the wild swans – the Whooper. This matches our familiar Mute Swan in size but is lighter in weight. It breeds in Arctic Russia and in Iceland, and is usually the Icelandic bird that we see in Britain and Ireland, most commonly in the west and north.

Despite the implications of its name, the Mute Swan can produce a variety of grunts and hisses, but these are only audible at close range. In contrast, the wild swans have the most wonderful trumpeting calls, audible for miles on a still day. The atmosphere of these spectacular cries set against the empty grandeur of the Arctic tundra and lakes where the birds breed is thrillingly captured by the Finnish composer Sibelius in *The Swan of Tuonela*.

The far-carrying calls of the Whooper Swan perform a vital function when, often in deteriorating autumn weather, families of swans gather to migrate south. The overseas journey from Iceland to northern Scotland is about 1000km (620 miles), many flying hours even on a swan's powerful wings and at a typical wind-assisted speed of about 120kph (75mph). Some of the journey may be made after dark, or in fog, and the calls help to keep the flock together, preventing the inexperienced youngsters from getting lost on the way. The swans may even travel in cloud, for some have been spotted on aircraft-control radar migrating from Iceland at the staggering height of 26,000ft: their identity and altitude were confirmed by the startled pilot of a passing aircraft diverting specially to check!

Flying at such a height may have pragmatic advantages. The huge effort required for this type of migration demands a tremendous amount of energy consumption – with a consequent risk of the body overheating. As birds cannot sweat to reduce their bodily warmth, the low temperature so high above the earth must have very positive benefits, and the jet-stream tail-wind speed assisting their passage is also likely to be at its greatest.

Thus can be summarized the endless variety of the aesthetic and biological fascination of birds and their lives. But wide though our knowledge may appear, just as intriguing is the realization that much more yet remains to be discovered, even about birds as widespread and numerous – even commonplace – as the Dunnock and Skylark. These are the foundations on which birdwatching enjoyment, and fulfilment, will always continue to be based.

Index

Acorn Woodpecker, 110
adaptive radiation, 18–19
Aepyornis, 16–17
Aepyornis titan, 16–17
Africa, 32, 35, 36, 42, 44, 62, 65, 83–4, 97, 100, 104, 107–9, 121, 124, 134, 147
agriculture, bird damage, 92–3, 152
air sacs, 73
Alauda, 18
albatrosses, 47, 63–4, 77, 140
Andes, 72
Anglesey, 90
Antarctic, 33, 49–50, 138, 145–6
Aquitaine, 19
Archaeopteryx, 8, 10, 11–13, 14–15
Archaeopteryx lithographica, 11
Arctic, 32, 33, 42, 43, 139–40, 155
Arctic Skua, 42, 43
Arctic Tern, 33, 41, 127, 153
Argentina, 42
Asia, 29, 71, 108
Atlantic Ocean, 31, 35, 63
auks, 15, 17, 29, 49, 52, 78, 126–7, 139, 142
Australasia, 33, 41, 42, 71
Auxerre, 13
Avocet, 64, 90

Babbler, 143
Baffin Island, 42
Bald Eagle, 23
Baptornis, 14
Bar-headed Goose, 31
Bar-tailed Godwit, 43, 88

Barn Owl, 69, 82
Barnacle Goose, 32, 91–2, 154
bats, flight, 20–1
Bavaria, 11–12
Bay of Biscay, 36
beaks, 64, 74–5, 78–9
Bearded Vulture, 108–9
Bee-eater, 51, 97, 118, 134, 143
Bee Hummingbird, 153
Bewick's Swan, 23, 92–3
bird-lime, 34
birds of paradise, 120
birds of prey, 16, 50, 52–3, 60, 66–7, 75, 78–83, 142
Black-faced Drioch, 104
Black-headed Gull, 27, 105, 106, 130, 151–2
Black Grouse, 123
Black Heron, 83–4
Black-tailed Godwit, 88
Black Tern, 76
Blackbird, 27, 64, 67–8, 100, 106, 107, 121, 126, 128–9, 136, 146, 149, 154
Blackcock, 123
blood circulation, 71
Blue Tit, 100, 107–8, 116–17, 124, 135–6, 137, 149, 151, 152
bones *see* skeleton
Bosporus, 35, 62
brain, 65
Brazil, 41, 42
breathing, 72–3
breeding, 114–49
    chicks, 141–9
    clutch size, 135–6
    co-operative breeding, 143
    colonies, 127–8

food supply, 136–7
    eggs, 114–19, 128
    incubation, 137–41
    migrants, 124
    nests, 128–35
    plumage, 120–1, 122–3
    song, 120–2
    territory, 120, 122, 125–7
Brent Goose, 92
British Museum, 11
British Trust for Ornithology, 39
brood patch, 137–8
Brown Pelican, 77
Budgerigar, 111
Bullfinch, 70, 98, 103, 152, 154
buntings, 16, 18, 23, 28, 122
Burry Inlet, 89
Buzzard, 56, 62, 79

Cambridge, 14
camouflage, 23, 117, 122, 130
Canada, 42, 90
Cape Pigeon, 77
Capercaillie, 57–8, 154
Carmine Bee-eater, 109
carnivorous birds, 17–18
Cattle Egret, 85
Cenozoic era, 9
Cetti's Warbler, 96
Chaffinch, 54, 131–2
Charadriiformes, 15, 16
chickens, 57, 60
chicks, 141–9
    camouflage, 130
    feeding, 143–8
    hatching, 141–2
    leaving the nest, 142–3
Chiff-chaff, 30, 35

China, 42
Chinstrap Penquin, 50
claws, 52–3, 79
co-operative breeding, 143
Collared Dove, 29–30
colonies, 127–8
colour: eggs, 117–18
    feathers, 23
Common Gull, 105, 151–2
Common Scoter, 78
Common Tern, 33, 41
Coot, 52, 131
copulation, 69–70
Cormorant, 48–9, 52, 55, 78,
    85, 130, 142
Corn Bunting, 68, 121
courtship feeding, 124
crakes, 52
cranes, 24, 35, 130, 155
Cretaceous, 13–15
crop, 70
Crossbill, 29, 64, 103, 137
crows, 16, 64, 105
Cuckoo, 16, 36, 128, 135, 137,
    147
Curlew, 88

dabbling ducks, 58, 93–4
Dalmatian Pelican, 86, 153
Dartford Warbler, 96
Darwin, Charles, 109
Darwin's Finches, 109
Denmark, 39
Diatryma, 17–18
digestion, 70–1
Dinornis maximus, 17
Dipper, 28, 53–4, 55, 154
displays, breeding, 123
diving, 48–50, 77–8
diving birds, 14–15, 52, 119,
    139
diving ducks, 48, 58, 94
Dotterel, 43
Dover, 151
doves, 34, 118
down feathers, 24–5
drinking, 111–13
ducks: chicks, 142, 143, 146
    eggs, 117, 137
    feeding, 93–5
    feet, 52
    mating, 70
    migration, 31, 124

nests, 130
plumage, 122
voices, 72
wings, 58
Dunlin, 68, 90, 155
Dunnock, 107, 117, 143, 147,
    154, 155
dust-bathing, 26

eagles, 52, 57, 78–9
ears, 67–9
egg teeth, 141
eggs, 114–19, 128
    colour, 117–18
    hatching, 140–1
    incubation, 137–41
    shapes, 118–19
egrets, 52
Egyptian Vulture, 109
Eider Duck, 25, 78, 94–5, 143,
    155
Eleanora's Falcon, 34
Emberiza, 18
Emperor Penguin, 17, 138,
    145–6
Emu, 50, 71
Enaliornis, 14
Eocene period, 16, 17, 18
Euparkeria, 11
evolution, 8–19
eyes, 65–7

falcons, 52, 60, 79, 80–1
feathers, 22–7
    Archaeopteryx, 10, 13
    breeding plumage, 120–1,
        122–3
    colours, 23
    flight feathers, 56–7
    functions, 22–3
    growth, 25
    moulting, 26–7, 122
    numbers of, 23
    preening, 24, 26
    structure, 24
    types, 23, 24–5
feeding, 74–113
    birds of prey, 78–85
    chicks, 143–8
    courtship feeding, 124
    drinking, 111–13
    insect eaters, 95–7
    omnivores, 104–8

plant eaters, 97–104
sea birds, 75–8
terrestrial flesh eaters, 95
tool users, 109
waders, 87–91
wildfowl, 91–5
woodpeckers, 110–11
feet, 52–3, 78–80
Fieldfare, 32
finches, 81, 146
    body temperature, 72
    eggs, 118
    feeding, 102–3, 144
    migration, 28
    plumage, 23, 122
    wings, 58
Flamingo, 46–7, 51, 112–13
flight, 74
    bats, 20–1
    falcons, 60
    game birds, 60–2
    gliding, 63–4
    insects, 21–2
    muscles, 57–8
    reptiles, 20
    skeleton and, 46–7
    speed of, 154–5
    wings, 57
flower feeding birds, 99
flowerpeckers, 71
flycatchers, 25, 118
flying lizards, 13
flying squirrels, 13
food supply, and breeding,
    136–7
    see also feeding
fossils, 8–9, 10–19
France, 13, 19, 34
frigate birds, 76
fruit-eating birds, 100–2
Fulmar, 63, 77, 148–9

Galapagos Islands, 109
Gallornis, 13
game birds, 16, 60–2, 130
Gannet, 26, 29, 52, 57, 63, 64,
    76, 77–8, 126–7, 130, 137,
    138, 142
Garden Warbler, 121
geese, 31, 32, 35, 81, 91–3, 124,
    137, 152
Gentoo Penguin, 50
geology, 8–9

Giant Petrel, 77
Gibraltar, Straits of, 35, 62
Giraldus Cambrensis, 91–2
gizzard, 70
gliding, 63–4
godwits, 18, 90
Goldcrest, 135, 154
Golden Eagle, 26, 62, 79, 125,
    127, 131, 137, 141, 142
Golden Oriole, 135
Golden Plover, 81, 90
Goldeneye, 129
Goldfinch, 102, 103, 131
Goliath Heron, 83
Goosander, 94, 117
Goshawk, 146
Great Australian Bight, 41
Great Bustard, 153
Great Northern Diver, 48
Great Skua, 42, 43, 76, 127
Great Spotted Woodpecker, 30,
    110, 111, 133
Great Tit, 54, 95, 135–6, 137
Greater Black-backed Gull, 37,
    88
grebes, 14, 52, 130–1, 139
Green Woodpecker, 110–11
Greenfinch, 102
Greenland, 32, 35, 42–3, 124
Greenland Wheatear, 32, 35
Grey Heron see Heron
Grey Plover, 87, 90
Greylag Goose, 91
grouse, 81
Guillemot, 29, 78, 118, 119,
    129–30
Gulf Stream, 32
gulls, 85
    beaks, 64
    chicks, 142
    eggs, 119, 137, 139
    evolution, 15
    feeding, 105–6, 151–2
    feet, 52
    nests, 126–7, 130
    wings, 58

Haberlein, Friederich Karl, 11
harriers, 79, 80
Hawfinch, 64, 102–3
hawks, 52, 60, 79, 81
head, 64–5, 74–5
hearing, 67–9, 121

heart, 71
Heligoland traps, 39
Heron, Grey, 26, 52, 55, 64, 70,
    83, 127–8, 131, 142, 148
herons, 24, 25, 62, 83–5
Herring Gull, 88, 105, 106, 148,
    151
Hesperornis, 14–15
Himalayas, 32
Hoatzin, 13
Hobby, 59, 60, 80
homing instinct, 38–9
Hoopoe, 60
House Martin, 38, 44, 51, 132
House Sparrow, 26, 46, 99, 121,
    132, 154
hummingbirds, 23, 58, 72, 99,
    116

Iceland, 32, 35, 155
Ichthyornis, 15
incubation, 137–41
insectivorous birds, 95–7
insects, flight, 21–2
internal organs, 69–71
Ireland, 30, 32, 60, 91–2, 139,
    155
irruptions, 29

jacanas, 52
Jackdaw, 133
Jan Meyen Island, 43
Japan, 85
Jay, 101, 105, 117
Jurassic period, 11, 13, 20
juvenile plumage, 27

Kansas, 14, 19
Kent, 19
Kenya, 112
Kestrel, 66, 80, 82, 155
kidneys, 69
King Penguin, 50, 138
Kingfisher, 26, 51, 66, 117, 118,
    134, 139
Kittiwake, 29, 78, 127–8, 142
Knot, 32, 42
Kori Bustard, 109

Lammergeyer, 108–9
Lapwing, 33, 61–2, 87, 129,
    130, 146
larks, 18, 72

legs, 50–5, 79–80
Lesser Black-backed Gull, 106
Lesser Flamingo, 112–13
Lesser Whitethroat, 122
life span, 153–4
lift, flight, 57
'lily-trotters', 52
Linnet, 102
Little Auk, 103–4
Little Gull, 76
Little Stint, 90
London Zoo, 154
Long-eared Owl, 69, 82, 154
Long-tailed Tit, 132, 143
Los Angeles, 19
lungs, 73

Madagascar, 16–17
Magpie, 108, 117, 132
Mallard, 42, 91, 94, 153, 154
Manakin, 143
Manx Shearwater, 36–7, 41, 42,
    63, 78, 134, 154
Maoris, 17
marsh terns, 130
Marsh Tit, 133
martins, 58–9
mating, 69–70
Meadow Pipit, 28, 40, 54, 81
Mediterranean Sea, 34, 35, 62
Merlin, 80–1
Mesozoic era, 9
Mexico, Gulf of, 14
Meyer, Hermann von, 11
migration, 28–45, 124
    navigation, 35–8
    radar-tracking, 40–1
    ringing, 39–40, 41–4
    weather and, 31–3, 34–5
Miocene period, 17, 18
mist nets, 39–40
'mistletoe-birds', 71
Moa, 17
Moorhen, 52, 131, 143
moulting, 26–7, 122
muscles, flight, 57–8
Mute Swan, 51, 65, 92–3, 94,
    137, 153, 155
'mutton bird', 41

Nakuru, Lake, 112
navigation, 35–8
nests, 128–35

New Guinea, 120
New Zealand, 17, 153
Nigeria, 44
Night Heron, 84
Nightingale, 34, 68, 72–3, 121
Nightjar, 16, 25, 26, 96
noddies, 140
Norfolk, 29
North Africa, 29
North America, 15, 110
Norway, 124
Nuthatch, 18, 53, 55

Okhotsk, Sea of, 44
Olduvai Gorge, 19
omnivorous birds, 104–8
oropendolas, 134
Osprey, 80
Ostrich, 16, 50, 58, 71, 72, 109,
    116, 117, 153
Outer Hebrides, 149
ovaries, 69
owls: brood sizes, 141
    eggs, 117, 118, 137
    evolution, 16
    eyesight, 66–7
    feeding, 81–3, 136
    feet, 52
    hearing, 68–9
    nests, 133
Oystercatcher, 88–9, 130, 153

Pachydyptes, 17
Pacific Ocean, 15, 109
Palaeocene period, 16
Paleotringa, 15
Palaeozoic era, 9
Pallas's Warbler, 42
Pappenheim, 11
parrots, 75
Partridge, 60–1, 62, 130
Passeriformes, 16, 53, 54–5,
    118, 141
pelicans, 52
pellets, 70, 83
penguins, 16, 17, 49–50, 78, 138
perching, 54–5
Peregrine, 60, 80–1, 127
petrels, 16, 76
phalaropes, 52, 77, 90–1
Pheasant, 130
pigeons, 34, 70, 137, 139
Pintail, 94

plant-eating birds, 97–104
Pliocene period, 18
plumage see feathers
plunge diving, 77–8
Pochard, 43–4, 94
Poor Will, 72
population fluctuations, 29
powder down, 25, 26
preen gland, 26
preening, 24, 26
primary feathers, 56–7
prions, 77
Proterosuchia, 10
Pseudosuchia, 10–11
Ptarmigan, 31
Pteranodon, 20
pterosaurs (pterodactyls), 20,
    21
Puffin, 29, 46, 49, 75, 76, 78,
    134
Punic Wars, 38–9
Purple Heron, 83
Purple Sandpiper, 89

Quaternary period, 19
Quelea, 104

radar-tracking migrants, 40–1
rails, 52
Rancho La Brea, 19
raptors, 35
Raven, 125–6, 127, 137
Razorbill, 29, 78
Red-backed Shrike, 97, 118
Red-breasted Merganser, 94
Red-footed Falcon, 80
Red Grouse, 60–1
Red-necked Phalarope, 90–1,
    139–40
Red-throated Diver, 154
Redpoll, 102
Redshank, 18, 87, 142
Redwing, 32
Reed Bunting, 123
Reed Warbler, 135
reptiles, 10–11, 20–21, 114
Rhea, 16
Rhinoceros Auklet, 15
rictal bristles, 25
Ring Ousel, 81
Ringed Plover, 43, 68, 87, 117,
    130
ringing, 39–40, 41–4

Robin, 27, 54, 55, 65, 106, 107,
    120, 154
Roc, 17
Rock Pipit, 30
Rocky Mountains, 42
Rome, 39
Rook, 27, 57, 105, 127–8, 154
Rough-Legged Buzzard, 51
Royal Albatross, 153
Ruff, 43, 123
Russia, 43, 155

Sahara Desert, 35, 107
St Kilda, 149
Sand Grouse, 111–12
Sand Martin, 118, 134
Sanderling, 87
sandpipers, 15
Sapsucker, 110
sawbill ducks, 91, 94
Scandinavia, 32, 35
Scotland, 124, 127, 139, 155
sea, food source, 75–8
sea birds, 48
    flight, 63–4
    migration, 28–9
sea ducks, 94–5
secondary feathers, 57
Sedge Warbler, 107
seed-eating birds, 75, 102–4
Shag, 48–9, 52, 78
shearwaters, 78
Sheldduck, 143
Sheppey, Isle of, 19
Short-eared Owl, 136
Shoveler, 64, 93
shrikes, 97
Sibelius, Jean, 155
Siberia, 31, 42
Siskin, 102
Sitta, 18
skeleton: Archaeopteryx, 12–13
    diving, 48–50
    and flight, 46–7
    fossils, 19
    limbs, 50–1
    wings, 55–6
skimmers, 77
Skokholm Bird Observatory, 37
skuas, 76, 139
skull, 64–5, 74–5
Skylark, 33, 40, 155
smell, sense of, 38, 65

Smoky Hill, Kansas, 14, 15, 19
Snipe, 43, 88, 90
Snowdon, 105
Solnhofen, 11
Song of Solomon, 38
Song Thrush, 64, 67–8, 122, 136
songs, 68, 72–3, 120–2
Sooty Falcon, 34
South Africa, 11, 42, 104
South America, 13, 15, 43, 100, 134
South-east Asia, 42
Spain, 34
sparrow family, 16
Sparrowhawk, 26, 79–80, 81, 146–7, 149, 155
speed of flight, 154–5
Spitzbergen, 43
Spoonbill, 52, 85–6
Spotted Flycatcher, 42, 96–7
Spotted Redshank, 87
Squacco Heron, 84–5
Starling, 10, 28, 32, 38, 41, 66, 100, 154
Stilt, 51
Stock Dove, 117, 133
Stonechat, 128–9
storks, 35, 57, 62
Storm Petrel, 76–7
Sulphur-crested Cockatoo, 154
Sunbird, 99, 134
Swallow, 32, 38–9, 40, 42, 44, 58–9, 111, 142, 154
swans, 24, 39, 70, 75, 92–3, 130
Swift, 16, 25, 32, 42, 51, 59, 80, 96, 111, 117, 118, 137, 139, 144–5, 153, 154
syrinx, 72–3

tails, 10, 53
talons, 52–3, 79–80
tanagers, 101
Tanzania, 19
Tawny Owl, 67, 82, 143

Teal, 94
teeth, *Archaeopteryx*, 10, 14–15
Temminck's Stint, 90
temperature, body, 71–2
terns, 15, 32, 33–4, 48, 58, 77, 126–7, 139, 140, 153
territory, breeding, 120, 122, 125–7
Tertiary period, 18–19
testes, 69
Thecodontia, 10
thermals, 62
thrushes, 36, 58, 81, 87, 102, 118, 154
tits, 54, 81, 118, 133, 146, 154
toes, 51, 52–3
tool users, 109
toucans, 101
Touraco, 13
traps, ringing birds, 39–40
Tree Pipit, 118
Treecreeper, 53, 55, 95–6, 154
Triassic period, 10–11
Tringa, 15
Trumpeter Swan, 153
Tufted Duck, 43, 94
Tufted Puffin, 15
Turkey (country), 29
Turnstone, 42, 43, 89–90
Turtle Dove, 29, 30, 38

United States of America, 14, 17

Volterra, 39
vultures, 53, 66, 72, 108–9

waders: beaks, 64, 75
chicks, 142–3
eggs, 117, 119, 137, 139
eyesight, 66
feeding, 86, 87–91, 95
feet, 52
migration, 124
nests, 130

fossils, 15
migration, 31, 32
wings, 58
wagtails, 118
Wales, 36–7, 89, 90, 105
Wandering Albatross, 153
warblers, 30–1, 32, 34, 36, 58, 96, 106–7
waterfowl, 16, 48, 93–5
Water Rail, 48, 52
weather, and migration, 31–3, 34–5
weaver birds, 104, 134
webbed feet, 52
weight, 153
Wheatear, 32
White, Gilbert, 44
White-fronted Goose, 43
White Pelican, 86
White Stork, 154
Whitethroat, 96
Whooper Swan, 92–3, 155
Whydah, 147
widow birds, 121
Wigeon, 43, 93
Wild Turkey, 153
wildfowl, 91–5
Willow Tit, 133
Willow Warbler, 26, 39, 96, 132
Wilson's Petrel, 103–4
wings, 55–64
falcons, 60
feathers, 56–7
game birds, 60–2
gliding, 63–4
Woodcock, 88, 90, 129
Woodpecker Finch, 109
woodpeckers, 16, 53, 110–11, 117, 118, 133, 137, 139
Woodpigeon, 33, 70, 99–100, 111, 146, 153, 154
Wren, 126, 129, 132, 147
Wyoming, 17

Yellowhammer, 28